Live 2 Tell (A Day in 'da Life)

Bles Shakur

Published by Bles Shakur, 2016.

This is a work of fiction. Similarities to real people, places, or events are entirely coincidental.

LIVE 2 TELL (A DAY IN 'DA LIFE)

First edition. November 7, 2016.

Copyright © 2016 Bles Shakur.

ISBN: 979-8215026489

Written by Bles Shakur.

Life Story Publications Presents...

1

Live 2 Tell

Bles Shakur

This is a work of fiction. Any references or similarities to actual events, real people, living, or dead, or to real locales are intended to give the novel a sense of reality. Any similarity in other names, characters, places, and incidents is entirely coincidental.

Cover concept by: Bles Shakur & Zachary Diaz

Cover layout and graphic design by: Zachary Diaz

Typesetting: Marcial F. Rivera & Tammy Rivera

Editor: Marcial F. Rivera & Tammy Rivera

Live 2 Tell: A novel by Bles Shakur

For complete copyright information, visit: www.lifestorypublications.com[1]

Life Story Publications

P.O. Box 1832, Sumter, SC 29151

Copyright © 2016 by Bles Shakur. All rights reserved. No part of this book may be reproduced in any form without the permission from the publisher, except by reviewer who may quote a brief passage to be printed in a newspaper or magazine.

Dedication

This book is dedicated to:
My family, my supporters, LaKeith Leonard (RIP), Matthew Horace (RIP), Michelle Beard (RIP), and to Tupac Amaru Shakur.
Love Is Always Love!!

Prologue

ON ANY OTHER Saturday night, University Avenue would be alive with traffic and people on the street, as if it was a parade. But for some strange reason, on this Saturday night, University Avenue was completely dead.

The only sounds of life that could be heard were coming from Club Platinum City, which sat on the corner of University and 112th Street. Logik and his best friend Banks were standing in front of the stage inside of Club Platinum City, enjoying the show that the four exotic dancers were putting on for the crowd.

Banks looked at Logik, "These bitches turning up in here tonight homey!" He shouted over the music as the strippers were leaving the stage. "Hell yeah! I ain't never seen this many people up in this muthafucka before!" Logik agreed. The club's capacity was only 270 people, but it was damn near 400 people packed inside of Platinum City on this particular night. Logik and Banks were sweating like some runaway slaves.

"A'ight, fellas. I want ya'll to dig real deep in your pockets for this next act. Coming to the stage is a very beautiful young lady who will have every man in this club, including myself, drunk off of her performance. So fellas, we present to you the lovely, Champagne!" Announced the DJ as he threw his headphones back on.

The DJ pressed a button and T-Pain's song, "I'm In Love With A Stripper" filled the club, and Champagne seductively paraded on stage. She placed both hands on top of her head, and started grinding her hips slowly to the beat. Her eyes were locked on Logik the whole time as she performed her act.

Champagne walked to the edge of the stage, dropped down and started popping her ass in front of Logik. Then she laid down on her back, grabbed both of her ankles and spread her legs wide-open. Exposing her fat pussy lips.

Logik made it shower twenty dollar bills on the stage and on Champagne as she worked the pole gracefully and seduced the crowd. He was caught up in a trance when she closed her eyes and started moving her body like a snake. "Damn," was all Logik could say as he watched this mysterious woman perform her magic on stage.

Then all of a sudden, both of her eyes turned solid white. Logik started to say something to Banks about it but he changed his mind, figuring that the alcohol and the pills he popped earlier had him seeing things. He tried to ignore her funny looking eyes and enjoy the show, but when a black hole appeared on her forehead and blood starting oozing out of it, Logik jumped back, almost losing his balance.

The show was now over as far as he was concerned. He turned towards Banks, "Yo, you see that —" He stopped in mid-sentence when he looked at Banks, who also had white eyes and was looking at him, smiling. A confused look appeared on Logik's face. "What the fuck!" he said as he started backing away from the stage.

Logik reached for his gun but was disappointed when he realized he left it in his car. He turned around to leave the club, but bumped right into Big E, who also had white eyes and blood all over his body. He pushed Big E aside, then started squeezing through the crowd and shoving people away as he went. Everybody he made eye contact with seemed to have the same solid white eyes and disgusting looking wounds on their bodies that were bleeding.

Logik pushed through dozens of people and still seemed not to be getting any closer to the exit. The shit that he was witnessing reminded him of an episode out of the Twilight Zone. All he wanted to do at that time was make it back to his car, and get as far away from Club Platinum City as possible.

A hand grabbed Logik's shoulder and he spun around with his guard up ready to swing it out with whoever, but when he saw who it was standing before him, with those same white eyes and blood oozing out of her neck, it was as if everything in the room had stopped moving. It was his girlfriend Jazmine. He starting shaking his head from side to side and backed away from her.

"No...No...Hell, No!" He turned around and ran towards the exit. When he reached the door, he snatched it open, only to find three masked men standing there as if they were waiting on him. One of the masked men raised his arm and aimed the gun directly at Logik's face. "Game Over," said the man, right before he squeezed the trigger. POW!

"Arrwwhh!" Logik awoke screaming and drenched in sweat. He was having another one of those nightmares.

Chapter 1

"MY LITTLE COUSIN getting money now." Peanut said to his cousin Logik. Logik just looked at him with a confused look on his face and shook his head.

Peanut was one of Logik's older cousins. Peanut had just come home from serving an eight year bid for armed robbery. While Peanut was in the pen, a few cats he knew had been hyping him up and telling him that is cousin Logik was doing "big things" on the street. But in reality, Logik was on the come-up and was only working with a little over two bricks at the time.

"Whut'chu mean, gettin' money now?" he asked. "I been out here doing me before you went in fool."

"Yeah, but not like this. Niggaz been telling me on the inside that you was out here laying major bricks nigga."

Logik grabbed the lighter off of the coffee table and lit the blunt that was hanging between his lips. He took a long drag, inhaled deeply, and blew out a cloud of smoke. "That's why it's not good to believe everything you hear."

Peanut wasn't trying to hear all that. He figured that Logik had to be playing with at least ten bricks. So he decided that he was going to continue to press Logik until he got what he came for. Peanut hadn't even gone to see his child or his mother. The first place he went as soon as he stepped outside of the prison gates was to Logik's apartment.

"Come on, family. Don't fade me out like that. Let me get a couple of them bricks you got so I can get myself together."

"A couple of them bricks!" Logik had to laugh at that one. "Bro, I don't know where you be getting your information from, but whoever been telling you shit about me in prison sure been feeding you a bunch of lies. I been out here taking loss after loss, and really, I'm just starting to get myself together. I understand you just coming home and everything, so that's why I'mma hit you off with a couple of ounces so you can make it do what it do. But all that brick nonsense you talking, I don't know a damn thing about that." said Logik, passing Peanut the blunt.

Logik's girlfriend Jazmine came walking into the living room, dressed in a slim fitted, cream-colored pantsuit. *And he claiming he don't got it like that. Look at the shit he got his girl wearing.* Peanut thought to himself, as he eyed Jazmine hungrily.

"Baby, you seen that diamond necklace with the pink in it that you gave me for my birthday?" Jazmine asked. She knew exactly where her necklace was at. It was right on top of the dresser in their bedroom. She just needed an excuse to walk into the living room and confirm who she already suspected it was that Logik was talking to.

Grimy-ass Peanut.

Jazmine knew that Peanut was supposed to be getting out of prison that year, she just didn't know when. After what Peanut did to Logik in the past, Jazmine stopped liking the boy. Even though he was Logik's cousin, Jazmine couldn't understand how he still could fuck with Peanut after he stole that $2,000 from Logik years ago, which was all the money that he had at that time. She didn't like Peanut's ass, and she really didn't like the way that he was now staring at her.

"No, I didn't see it Jazmine, but you need to find it because I paid too much money for that necklace for you to be losing it like that."

Jazmine put her hand on her hip and looked at Logik like he was crazy. "Boy, shut up." she scolded him and then turned to walk back into the bedroom.

"Jazmine!" Logik called after her. Jazmine stopped in her tracks then turned and faced him. "What!" she yelled in an aggravated tone.

"Come here for a second." Jazmine came walking back into the living room. "I know he done put on a few pounds and got this big ass beard like he Rick Ross or summin. But, you know who this is, right?" Logik asked, gesturing with his head towards Peanut.

How could I forget? Better yet, how could you forget? She said in her mind. "Yeah, I know exactly who he is." replied Jazmine, before she turned back around and headed down the hallway.

"I see, Jazmine still tripping about that money I stole from you back in the day?" He shook his head like he was disappointed. "Dog, that shit is ancient history now. Besides, I took that bread from you, not her." Peanut explained, feeling somewhat embarrassed.

Logik just shrugged his shoulders.

Peanut turned in his seat to face Logik. "Listen, little cousin. Back in them days my head been kind of messed up. That was some crab shit I did to your family. But, as soon as I get back on my feet, I'mma pay you that money back, plus interest." He passed Logik the blunt back.

"Jazmine the only one still on it like that. I'm not even sweating it. It wasn't like you physically took it from me. You just was on your coked up jack boy shit back then. But me and Banks caught you, and pounded you out for that shit that same week." Logik reminded him. "But like you said, that's ancient history now."

Peanut remembered that day well. And honestly, he still felt some type of way about the ass whupping he received. "Yeah, that's wassup. But yo, wassup with some of them bricks my nigga?"

He looked at Peanut like he had shit on his face.

"You must not be hearing me nigga. I told your ass that them rumors you been hearing about me been some bullshit. Don't you think if I been moving that type of work, that I would have been had me a house built somewhere instead of living in this apartment nigga?" Logik asked. He saw the look of disbelief on Peanut's face, which was starting to annoy him.

"Yo, look. You want these 41/2 ounces I got for you or not?" asked Logik. He didn't like the vibes that he was getting from Peanut. He just hoped that he didn't have to lay Peanut's ass to rest down the line, because at the end of the day, *once a grimy nigga, always a grimy nigga.*

Peanut saw that Logik wasn't going to give him the type of work he really wanted, so he decided to stop pressing the issue and just take the free 41/2 ounces.

"It's all good cousin. I'll take the 41/2 that you got for me."

Logik shook his head. "Yeah, a'ight. I don't keep my shit here though. Just let me know where you gonna be at around 7 or 8 tonight and I'll just drop the shit off to you. Me and Jazmine about to head out to this fashion show that her sister got going on for her clothing line she promoting." Logik explained.

Yeah, whatever. You getting all this money, but you wanna birdfeed me like I'm a sucker or something. But it's all good though. You and your bitch can jump off of a bridge somewhere for all I care. Peanut thought to himself with hatred in his heart.

"Bet."

Peanut gave Logik a handshake and a hug before he left.

THE NEXT DAY, Logik was cruising down the interstate in his silver Lexus LS-400. He got off on the upcoming exit then made a right turn at the traffic light. 15 minutes later, he was turning down one of the blocks that two of his young gunners operated on.

Once a week, like clockwork, Logik would hit his two young soldiers off with a package to sell. His young gunners always ran through the packs each week like Usain Bolt. Sometimes he had to get on their asses about moving the work too slow, but for the most part, the young gunners completed their weekly objectives and always came correct with his bread.

Logik pulled up in front of the young gunner's trap house and tapped the horn twice. Seconds later, both of his young soldiers came out of their trap and hopped into the Lexus.

"What's poppin', Logik?" Marcus spoke, reaching over to give Logik some dap.

"You." Logik replied. "Budda, what's da bizness young soldier?"

"I'm maintaining, big bro." Budda replied.

"A'ight, so what we looking like this week?" Logik asked. "I got some more moves to make, so let's take care of this bizness here pronto."

Marcus pulled a wad of cash out of his right pocket and handed it to Logik. Then Budda did the same.

"That's four and four right there." Budda said, referring to the bread he and Marcus handed Logik.

Each week, Logik gave Budda and Marcus 41/2 ounces of coke, which he expected $3600 from each of them every Sunday. A little baking soda, water, and heat would easily turn the 41/2 to 6 ounces of cook up. They each profited $2500 or more each week after Logik's cut was set aside.

Marcus lit a cigarette then looked at Logik.

"Yo big bro. Some bullshit happened to me about two weeks ago down the block dog. I fucked 'round and got caught slipping. I been -."

He cut Marcus off in mid-sentence. "Don't tell me you got bagged by a five-o and ain't let me know?" Logik seriously inquired.

"Naw naw, ain't nuttin' like that." Marcus cleared his throat before he started back speaking. "Two older heads I ain't never seen before whipped out on me and got me for a zone and a lil' over a band." He explained. Marcus got heated even talking about the situation.

Logik had a confused and menacing look on his face. "And where the fuck was Budda when all this was taking place?" He looked at Budda then back to Marcus.

"Shit, I was in the trap when that shit was going on. This nigga." Budda pointed to Marcus. "Mack daddy muthafucking Marcus, left the trap chasing some big butt bitch who was walking down the block. A few minutes later, I heard car tires skidding off and shit. Thinking this fool in trouble or summin. I grabbed the TEC-9 off the table and walked down the block to find this fool." He tilted his head toward Marcus. "Laying on the ground snoring like my grandpops and shit." Budda wanted to get a laugh when he finished but felt that the time wasn't appropriate, so he held his giggles inside.

Logik clenched his jaw and scratched the side of his face. "What I wanna know is, how them muthafuckers got the drop on you?" He asked confusedly. "You been strapped wasn't you?"

Budda interjected. "Oh, yeah, that's another thing. This nigga left his strap laying on the table next to mines chasing after that chick." Budda shook his head and chuckled.

Marcus slowly started rubbing his hand on the side of his face, disappointed in himself.

"Yeah, I got caught slipping. I fucked up. But yo, if I ever see them dudes again, I don't give a fuck where it's at. I'm popping off!" Marcus angrily shouted with venom in his voice.

Logik shook his head in disgust. "Well, at least you ain't let that lil' incident stopped you from not having my bread that week." Logik paused. "But yo, how these niggaz look that caught you slipping Marcus?"

He flicked the cigarette butt out of the window before he spoke. "The dude that had the gun pointed at my face was a brown-skinned dude with yellow ass eyes, and a long ass scar on the side of his face. The other mufucka been this short, stocky, dark-skinned nigga."

The thumping bass notes from a passing car rattled the Lexus as it passed by. A woman and a man who looked to be crackheads were walking towards the trap. Logik spotted them and decided it was time he left so he could handle some other relevant business.

"Yo, here the 9 piece, go." He handed Marcus a folded yellow envelope which contained nine ounces of cocaine on the inside for Marcus and Budda. "Them two muthafuckers you described that robbed you, Marcus. I'mma run their description by my sources in the street and see if we can locate them fools."

Logik then nodded toward the crackheads who stopped in front of the trap and looked toward his car. The crackheads reminded Logik of them zombies off of the movie called, Land of the Dead. "Listen, let me go do me, and ya'll niggaz stay focused, and stop muthafucking slipping out here in these streets."

Marcus cuffed the envelope as he and Buddha got out.

Logik wound the window down before he pulled off. "Oh yeah. Don't mention nuttin' to nobody about what happened to Marcus neither. Ya'll already know we move in silence. If them niggaz that got Marcus be some local niggaz, then we'll find them fools in no time."

Chapter 2

A FEW HOURS later, the hot North Carolina sun was replaced by a clear blue-black night sky. The sounds of the city and cries of the streets filled the air.

Logik, Banks, and Black were sitting in Banks' Navigator which was parked in Ms. Pat's front yard. Banks and Black were Logik's childhood friends. Ms. Pat was a long-time local old-school hustler since the 70's. For many years, she bootlegged liquor and ran poker parties every Sunday night. Her yard would look like a club parking lot, with cars parked and people standing around everywhere.

Her neighbors had become immune to the profane language, traffic, and loud music that went on every Sunday night. Hell, some of the neighbors were always present each Sunday at Ms. Pat's house, contributing to the rowdy atmosphere themselves. Word on the street had been that Ms. Pat had some kind of dirt on the Chief of Police, and that's why she was never seriously bothered by law enforcement over the years.

The sounds of Young Jeezy explaining why he needed a vacation pumped out of the speakers inside of Banks' Navigator.

Logik and Banks were laughing up a storm as they listened to another one of Black's wild-ass stories.

"...ya'll niggaz laughing, but I'm dead-ass serious. I mean, I thought Shorty had just liked it from the back because every time I stopped and tried to get her to turn over so I can hit it from the front, she started spazing out and shit and telling me to just keep hitting it from the back." He sneezed, then continued, "After thirty minutes of that, I said fuck all that and just turned her ass around. Now, I got my dick in my hand, about to slide up in Shorty, right? So summin told me to look down, right? Man! This chick's clit was half the size of my pinky nigga!" He explained, showing them his pinky finger.

Logik and Banks started laughing uncontrollably. As soon as they calmed down, Black continued, "Now keep in mind, I'm high as hell at the time, right? I'm on cush, I'm on that drink, and I just got finished popping a pill. So when I saw that shit between her legs, all type of evil thoughts started going through my mind at the time because at first, I actually thought she had some other shit going on down there."

Logik and Banks started laughing so hard, that they were out of breath and had tears running down their faces.

"She talking 'bout don't trip, Black. It ain't even what you think that is." Black wrinkled his nose with his eyebrow raised. "I'm like, it ain't what I think it is!" He said, mocking the girl's voice.

"Hold on one goddamn minute now! How you know shorty ain't been a man who done had one of them sex changes or some shit?" Banks teased. He knew that the girl Black described was a female. He just wanted to push Black's button.

"Don't play yourself, Banks. You don't think I know the difference between a dick and a jumbo-size clit fool?" Black hotly retorted defensively.

Logik chuckled, "Obviously you didn't, if you had to ask Shorty why she had a miniature dick between her legs!" Logik and Banks started laughing uncontrollably again.

A knock on the driver's-side window brought Black's story to an end.

"Wassup, Monique?"

"Logik still in here Banks? My momma want him." She stuck her head through the window trying to locate Logik inside the dark truck.

Banks put his hand on Monique's forehead and eased her face out of his truck.

"Yo, Monique. What the hell is your problem woman? You got your head all up in my shit inspecting like you five-o or summin."

She rolled her eyes ignoring Banks' sarcasm.

"Fuck you Banks. Logik, you in here babe?" She always liked Logik because she thought that he was good people. Even though she smoked her dope and maybe turned a trick every once in a while for a high. He never treated her like a crackhead…even though she was one.

"What up Monique?" Logik asked out loud, as he opened his phone to check an incoming text message.

"My momma said come inside for a minute, she need to speak with you." She said. Monique was Ms. Pat's crackhead daughter. Though the crack did affect her appearance, anyone with eyes could tell that Monique had been a beauty queen in her younger days.

Logik stepped out of the Navigator and headed towards the crowded front porch. Leaving Monique and Banks talking shit to each other as they often did.

A few young guys who Logik knew from the North Side of town were standing in a small group in Ms. Pat's yard talking loudly. As Logik was walking by, he noticed one of the dudes in the group staring daggers at him. The uncomfortable stare caused him to stare back at the dude viciously until the dude broke eye contact. *I don't know who the fuck that lil' nigga thought he be looking at. Lil' muthafuckas on the wrong side of town anyway.* Logik thought to himself as he squeezed through the small crowd on the front porch and walked into the packed house.

The inside of the house smelled like a mixture of alcohol, weed, and cigarette smoke. Logik spoke to several people he knew as he made his way towards the loud and intense poker game that was taking place in the kitchen.

There was a big round table in the kitchen and the eight chairs which sat around it was occupied by gamblers. The game that was being played was Texas Hold 'Em. Sky was the limit, which meant that any player could bet as much money as they wanted to bet. If the other player couldn't match the bet, he or she then had a choice to go All

In with whatever money they had left, or fold their hand and lose whatever money that they already had invested in the pot.

Ms. Pat was the "House Woman". Her duties were to collect 15% off of each pot, make sure she provided her players with free food and drinks, and finally, make sure that no one tried to cheat her or another player. Her two brothers, Gerald and Earl were always present as well. Their duties were to ensure that the game ran accordingly, collect and stash whatever money Ms. Pat randomly gave them throughout the night, and physically handle anybody who posed a threat.

Ms. Pat also had some wild-ass grandsons who she raised that always hung around her house with some of their South Side friends, so robbing Ms. Pat was out of the question.

Logik's mother and Ms. Pat had been real good friends for over 27 years before she passed away, which was 10 years ago. Leaving young Logik a motherless child.

"I bet $20 dollars," said the man with the dark shades on.

"Alright," a fat man replied. "I call your $20, and raise you $200." he said boldly, as he threw two bills in the nice-sized pot which sat in the middle of the table.

"Man, why the fuck is you betting so damn much?" The man wearing the dark shades asked furiously. He had already lost $700 that night.

"Look, I ain't got time for all that crying, Bobby. You gonna call the bet, or throw that shit in the deck?"

Bobby stood up. "Man, fuck you Earl. I don't know who the fuck you think you talking to like that!" He barked.

Ms. Pat decided it was time to calm the back and forth tongue wrestling down before shit got out of hand.

"Jimmy, honey, you know it ain't no reason to be carrying on like that. The rule is, sky is the limit. Now you and Earl ain't 'bout to start that bullshit up in here tonight goddammit!" Ms. Pat vexed.

When she looked up, she saw Logik talking to one of her nieces. She told her brother Gerald to hold things down until she got back.

"...please, boy. Let me leave you alone before somebody go and tell Jazmine I'm try'na holla at her man." Veronica said flirtatiously to Logik as they talked in the living room.

"Last time I checked, I been a grown ass man," Logik said, "plus, she already know that I'm like family to ya'll. She won't believe no shit like that anyway." He lied. He knew damn well that Jazmine would have believed the rumor.

Logik knew that Veronica had a big mouth and hung around too many females that Jazmine knew. So fucking Veronica was definitely out of the question.

Ms. Pat walked up.

"Veronica, go take your fast ass on somewhere. Me and Jermaine got some business to talk about." Ms. Pat told Veronica, referring to Logik by his government name.

"Dang, Auntee, you rude." Veronica said embarrassedly. "I'll talk to you later, Logik." She walked off, putting an extra switch in her hips, hoping that Logik was watching.

"Look at her," Ms. Pat told Logik, referring to Veronica. "That's all she wanna do, stay up in a man's face. You know she walking like that 'cause she hope you watching. But, anyways, come walk with me out to the barn in the back yard." She instructed. They squeezed through the cluttered kitchen and made it to the back door.

Once they walked inside the dark barn, Ms. Pat felt around in the darkness until she touched the string that hung from the light switch. She gave the string a tug and the inside of the barn immediately illuminated. The inside of her barn looked like Fred Sanford's junkyard.

She walked to the back of the barn and stopped in front of a tall steel cabinet. She then pulled a set of keys out of her housecoat and unlocked it.

Logik's eyes stretched in excitement when he saw Ms. Pat laying an assortment of guns out on the floor in front of him.

"I trust you, Jermaine. More than a lot of my own family. Now, I'll be lying if I told you that I knew how much any of this shit is worth. Hell, I can't even tell you what kind of guns some of these things is." She explained. "Now, Gerald and Robert got a few guns out in the country. So they ain't gonna buy 'em, and you know I ain't gonna sell them to just anybody. But, if you don't want 'em Jermaine, I'll just have to give 'em to Gerald or Earl. But if I can make summin off of these things, then that's even better."

"Where you get all this from, Ms. Pat?" He gestured towards the guns.

"You don't need to know all that information, Jermaine." She nonchalantly replied. "Let's just say somebody slipped, so I gripped."

"Nah, I ain't tryna get in your bizness or nuttin, Ms. Pat, but I asked you that because if them ain't no brand new guns, then it's a possibility that either one of them guns could have bodies on them, feel me?"

She scratched her wig, now understanding. "Oh, okay. I see what you mean, babe....well, I can't tell you what nobody done with nuttin'. You and my brothers the only ones that know about these guns."

"I'll give you $2200 for all of 'em, Miss Pat. I know you about bread."

"Hey, now! Somebody know Ms. Pat." she complimented herself when Logik stated the obvious. "But I'll take the $2200 babe, that's fine."

He pulled a small bankroll out of his pocket and counted out $2200 for Ms. Pat.

"I'mma come back and pick 'em up tomorrow sometime, but I'll call you before I just come over though."

"That's fine by me, Jermaine."

Logik started helping Ms. Pat put the guns back in the cabinet. She pulled the string on the light switch and they walked out.

Logik's cell phone vibrated in his pocket. He looked at the screen and saw that it was a call from Banks.

"What's good?"

"Yo, you got this nigga, Smurf right here tryna cop 21/2, but all I got is 11/2 on me and Black said he ain't re-up yet. You got a zone on you so I can get this nigga straight?"

"Yeah, I got that. Eh, yo, what Smurf that is? 'Cause you know I don't fuck with that fool, Smurf from Springdale?" Logik seriously inquired.

"Nah, bruh. This the nigga Smurf from Hillside Gardens."

Logik was now walking through the living room.

"Yo, I'm walking out the front door now." He hit End on his cell phone.

As soon as Logik made it to the bottom of the steps, the same young boy who was staring at him earlier was now staring daggers at him again. When Logik peeped it, he changed directions, then started walking towards the young boy.

"Is summin wrong wit'cho eyes my man?" Logik asked.

The youngster didn't back down.

"I ain't ya man, nigga. You betta get out of my face before I stretch your ass." He warned Logik.

"Before you do what!" Logik rushed towards him.

One of the young boy's friends stepped in between the two, trying to prevent shit from popping off.

Banks and Black turned their heads when they heard all the commotion going on. When they spotted Logik, they quickly exited the Navigator to aid and assist their homeboy.

A crowd started forming around the confrontation that was going on.

"Tell your homies to let you go so you can stretch me, nigga!" Logik challenged, still trying to fight the boy.

One of the dudes that was holding the young boy back saw Banks and Black walking up threateningly, so he reached into his fatigue jacket and whipped out a gun.

Click-Clack!

He jacked a round in the chamber and held the gun downwards.

"If y'all want action, y'all muthafuckas can get it. Real talk!" The young dude with the gun yelled nonchalantly.

Immediately, Logik, Black, and Banks simultaneously pulled their guns out. "You must wanna get ya self killed out here tonight, nigga!" Logik barked, ready to raise his arm and squeeze the trigger.

He really would hate to disrespect Ms. Pat's crib like that if it came down to it.

One of Ms. Pat's grandsons emerged from within the crowd of partygoers and stepped between the two groups when he witnessed how the situation quickly went from zero to sixty.

"Ain't shit 'bout to pop off in my grandmother's yard, period!" Ms. Pat's grandson, JuJu spazed out.

The young dude who had been giving Logik those evil stares, his name was Lil' E.

"Yo, Lil' E. Ya niggaz got shit twisted if ya'll think ya'll gone come over here on the South with that hot boy shit!"

Lil' E's eyes roamed the large group of Southsiders who basically had him and his homeboyz surrounded. Seeing that the odds would be against them if they did decide to pop off, Lil' E quickly calmed down.

"Nah, we ain't tryna disrespect your grandmother's crib JuJu," Lil' E pointed to Logik. "That nigga right there came at me first."

JuJu pointed to Logik. "That nigga right there like a big brother to me. If he came at you first, it had to be for a reason!"

"Oh, we on it like that, JuJu?" Lil' E asked, looking at JuJu menacingly.

JuJu ignored the question. "Yo, y'all got to get the fuck up out of my grandmother's yard with that shit, Lil' E." He responded nonchalantly.

The eyeboxing that ensued between JuJu and Lil' E got so intense, Logik gripped the P89 he held tighter, trying to restrain himself from putting the disrespectful youngster out of his misery.

Ms. Pat's grandsons and Lil' E had been somewhat cool with each other over the years, despite the 23 years of South Side/North Side history of hardship between each other.

Ms. Pat's house was the most known house in the urban ghetto of the South Side. Hell, her house had been notorious to all hoods throughout the city.

Logik knew that the beef between the South Side and North Side could spark again, and some of them young boyz from the North Side was to end up trying some dumb shit later on.

If the South and North Side beef start cooking again, due to a confrontation which initially sparked at Ms. Pat's house, then her house in the near future could become a potential crime scene for Homicide to investigate.

Lil' E started walking off with his crew, lowering the razor in his eyes, promising Logik and company a different outcome next time.

Chapter 3

THE RATTLING NOISE came from the other side of the house. Debating whether she left the back door open or not, Jazmine stopped folding Mrs. Tallwater's laundry and went to investigate.

The back door was locked shut.

She looked out the kitchen window, her eyes roamed over the whole backyard looking for anything out of the ordinary. Suddenly, the cordless phone that was in her back pocket started to ring.

Beep...Beep.

"Mrs. Tallwater's residence." Jazmine said answering the phone, trying to sound conservative.

"Bitch, you know your ass don't talk like that." Patience teased.

Jazmine chuckled, "Girl, shut up." She playfully replied after she realized who it was on the other end of the phone.

The batteries on Jazmine's cell phone were completely dead because she accidentally left the charger at home that morning before work. So Mrs. Tallwater's house phone became her temporary replacement...for that day, at least.

Jazmine was a nursing aide for Better Life Care Service. Mrs. Tallwater was one of their clients. She worked three days out of the week, from 8am to 5pm. Even though Logik wasn't hurting in the streets financially, and would buy her whatever she wanted. Being the independent person Jazmine had always been, she still chose to work. Not only so she wouldn't have to be cooped up in the house all day, but simply because that's what independent women do.

"Shoot, I had done gave up on you calling me back girl."

"Hmm, well one of my lil' friends came through to check up on me."

"Yeah, and that ain't all his ass did either." They both started giggling like high school girls.

"Heffa, you ain't never lied." Patience confessed.

Jazmine went to check on Mrs. Tallwater.

Mrs. Tallwater had fallen asleep in her wheelchair. Jazmine went and sat in the den for some privacy.

"Look, now go ahead and finish telling me about what happened with my babe at Ms. Pat's house last night." Jazmine inquired.

Patience went on to tell her about the events that took place the night before.

A cold feeling suddenly came over Jazmine.

"I don't know Jazmine. All I know is that I hope that North Side, South Side bullshit don't start back up again. Shoot, the niggaz don't know what that shit be affecting me and my girls to whenever we go out and bump heads with them North Side girls."

Jazmine started feeling depressed. She was not in the streets like Patience was, and she didn't play the club scene at all. She wasn't raised in the inner-city like Patience, so all the drama that came with living in the hood she never experienced.

Jazmine shook her head. "All of this shit crazy if you ask me. I been telling Logik he need to stop acting like he addicted to this damn city and we move out of state somewhere and start over," she took a deep breath, "I mean, me and Logik both smart and determined people, so it ain't no limits to what we could do when we both put our minds together. He just need to get away from here before he end up getting killed out here in these streets." Jazmine felt her eyes getting watery from the emotional build up, so she let Patience take over the conversation. Hoping that she would change the subject.

Patience was an associate of Jazmine. They met each other in high school and *somewhat* kept in contact with each other ever since. Patience was good for conversation and everything, but Jazmine really didn't trust the girl. Patience was known for fucking other women's men. Jazmine would never approve of Patience being around Logik *anywhere*, if she wasn't there to monitor them both.

Jazmine was 29 years old, a cocoa-complexioned, five foot six inch, goddess. Her high cheekbones complimented her exotic-looking face. She had the face and beauty of an ancient Egyptian queen. Her C-cup breasts, curvaceous body, and model strut, which made her ass jiggle with each step made men and most women turn their heads anytime she walked by.

She couldn't figure out for the life of her why Logik still chose to cheat on her like he did. And sometimes with females who weren't even as beautiful as she was.

She just couldn't understand the man.

On the other end of the phone, Patience was wondering, as she listened to Jazmine babble, on how it would be to have a man like Logik. *Shit, the boy got money, he fine as hell, plus I heard he got a big dick.* Patience said in her mind.

Patience had a crush on Logik. She always made sure that she was present at the majority of the events that went on in the city because she knew that there was a strong possibility that Logik would be there. She figured that the more she be in Logik's presence, then one day he might approach her on a sexual level (despite her and Jazmine's friendship). Logik's swag and his whole demeanor about himself always made Patience soak in her panties anytime she was around him.

Later that night, Jazmine laid naked in bed with her hand comfortably resting on Logik's bony chest after their long and sweaty sex session.

"I talked to patience today," Said Jazmine as she played with the soft curly hair at the bottom of Logik's stomach.

Logik was laying there in his boxer shorts with his right arm draped around Jazmine's shoulder. "Oh yeah? Wassup with her?" He asked, unconcerned.

She sighed.

"I can't believe you ain't told me about that shit that's happened at Ms. Pat's house."

"What do you mean? Why I ain't told you about what happened?" He quizzically asked. "What, you my parole officer or summin?" He hated talking to her about personal shit, even though he knew how loyal she was.

She smacked his flat stomach playfully. "Stop being funny, Logik. I'm serious though babe. You know I don't want to see anything happen to you out there in them streets. Now, I know you gotta be out there to make money for us and everything, but I been told you babe, that I'm not with you for money. Shoot, if I had to work by myself just to pay the bills, you know I wouldn't have no problem doing that. It's just that I don't want you to get kill out there by some of these wild-ass young boys, Jermaine."

"Look at me." He said, as she looked up at him pitifully. "Now, let me tell you summin. I watched my momma work in a sewing factory since I was five years old. I remember how tired she used to look when she got home. My Pops left when I was three, so a lot of the manly things needed to be done around the house and in the yard, she did that. And as soon as I was old enough to pick up a broom, I helped too." Water started to well up in his eyes. "My momma dies chasing some bullshit American Dream." He paused because tears started running down his face. He wiped the tears and continued, "When my momma died, her life insurance policy that was left to me was only worth twenty-five thousand dollars. But the type if funeral me and my aunt wanted to have for momma costed thirty thousand. She ain't even owned her own damn house when she died, Jazmine. She worked all them years chasing some damn American Dream. But guess what?" He asked, "That thirty thousand dollar funeral me and my aunt wanted to have for my momma? I made sure it happened! I took ten thousand dollars off of that life insurance policy and copped some work with it. And guess what Jaz? I ain't ever looked back yet."

"See, the problem with most black people is that they would rather bust their ass and work for the white man all their damn life and they satisfied with that, long as they got enough money to pay their bills with, they cool. A lot of them never even owned their own damn house! Now, tell me this Jazmine, you think these rich white muthafuckas in corporate America ever gotta worry about competing with a black person who is chasing that American Dream? Hell, nah!" He said before she could respond.

He slowly started running his fingers through her head.

"Me and you doing alright for ourselves, Jaz. The only thing we missing is our own business or businesses, our own land, and our own family. And I'd be damned if I work 30 or 40 years of my life just to get that either. Shit, around that time, me and you gone be old ass hell. Your pussy gone, always dry as hell, and I'mma need Viagra just to get on hard. Fuck that!" He preached.

She started laughing. In a way, what Logik had said made a lot of sense to her. She just didn't know if the risk of living the lifestyle of black competitors in America was worth death or Logik doing 25 years in prison.

Logik always knew how to make Jazmine feel good about any negative thoughts she may have. To her he was very intelligent, and she always loved the way his voice sounded.

His fingers that were slowly running through her hair and massaging her scalp were starting to make her extremely wet between the thighs again.

Before she knew it, her lips started kissing on Logik's chest, and eventually made its way to his sleeping anaconda, then round two of lovemaking began.

THE BRISK AUGUST night breeze swirled through the block, blowing trash tumbling across the street.

Whenever Logik wanted to "creep" incognito, he always borrowed Black's green Ford Explorer which Logik had a spare key to. The Explorer would always be parked in front of Black's father's house.

Logik had been creeping with this stripper chick named Champagne on and off for a few months now. He met her at the Car and Bike Show that summer. She ended up giving him her phone number after he informed her about his relationship with Jazmine.

Two weeks after the Car and Bike Show, he saw her again at a strip club called "Platinum City." He, Black, and Banks were standing in front of the stage with a wad of bills in their hands, sipping syrup and making it rain dollars on the three strippers that were on stage dancing.

After their performance, the club owner came on stage and introduced the next act.

Seconds later, a tall, thick, Amazon chick with a heart-shaped ass took the stage. Her face strongly favored that of the actress Megan Good. The only thing she had on when she came on stage was a pair of red ankle-strap Elizabeth & James high-heels.

Immediately, Logik recognized the sexy stripper on stage as the same chick he met at the Car and Bike Show.

Damn, Shorty a fucking stripper. He thought to himself.

Their eyes met as she danced exotically on stage. Her performance had the niggaz in front of the stage making it rain nothing less than twenty dollar bills. After her show was done, she went into the private dressing room that was marked Dancers Only to clean up and change into something less revealing.

When she came from out of the dancer's room, she went and sat at the bar. Her eyes scanned the club until she found who she was looking for.

Logik.

She waved Michelle (one of the sexy bartenders) over to the end of the bar where she sat. She whispered into her ear and then sent Michelle on her way.

"Excuse me, but the young lady over there," Michelle pointed to Champagne who sat with her legs crossed at the bar, "sent this bottle of Rosé over to you." She told Logik.

Two hours later, Logik had Champagne in the Holiday Inn with her model legs in the air, long-dicking her until her body shivered like an electrifying bolt of lightning was passing through it.

Meanwhile, Logik pulled Black's green Explorer into her drive-way and got out. Champagne opened the front door with her birthday suit on.

"Hey handsome," she said seductively.

"What's poppin', Ma?" He replied.

She pulled him into her house and started kissing him hungrily. The first kiss was a spark that ignited a lustful hunger from within. The second kiss was sloppy, wet, and animalistic.

"I want you to fuck me now, babe." She said aloud, as she quenched her sensual thirst with a taste of his lips.

He scooped her up in one swift motion and carried her over to the plush loveseat and laid Champagne on her back. He stripped naked, stood on the loveseat and dropped his dick into her mouth.

"Mmm." He moaned when she gripped his long, curved dick. She ran her tongue around the head before wrapping her lips around the shaft, then proceeded to devour his manhood greedily. He was on the verge of busting off in her mouth, so he pulled his dick out and stepped off of the couch. He went into his pocket to retrieve a Magnum condom. After he put the condom on, Champagne was lying on her back with both legs behind her head, exposing her huge pussy hole. His hand didn't need to assist his dick as it slid inside of her sloppy wet pussy hole with ease. She opened her legs wider, allowing him full access to her most private of possessions. He started slamming his dick inside of her like a madman. Champagne was throwing her pussy back on his dick, matching his aggression.

He put both hands under the bottom of her ass and pounded her pussy relentlessly, making her cum hard and himself even harder.

She went into the bathroom to clean herself up. After she was done, she brought Logik a washcloth lathered in soap so he could wash her juices off of his shaft. When he finished, he handed her the washcloth back, then she disappeared again. She came back into the living room with a Palma Dutch Masters cigar and a sack of Purple Haze in her hand. She handed Logik the cigar and he proceeded to roll up.

Champagne loved being a stripper because the money was good. She made more on Thursday and Sunday nights stripping than the average person made all month. She was single by all means and planned on remaining that way. But, she was willing to make an exception for Logik's long-dick ass if he ever wanted to upgrade their friendship.

He took three drags on the exotic weed then passed it to Champagne.

"Whut'chu got to eat up in this bitch, Ma?" He asked, as they sat on the loveseat.

She looked at him and licked her lips. "Me," she said seductively, referring to her pussy instead of the food he inquired about.

"Trust me, I would if you was my bitch. But on the real though, whut'chu got up that kitchen? Nigga hungrier than a muthafucka."

She passed him the blunt back, then blew out a cloud of smoke. "I was so busy that I ain't even had a chance to cook today, Boo. I'm sorry." She replied apologetically. "You want me to go out and get you summin from the Waffle House or summin?" She felt weird how she was treating Logik like her man, but she couldn't help herself. She was feeling high.

He shook his head. "Nah, you alright. You got some cereal and milk up in that bitch though?"

Her eyebrow raised. "Cereal and milk at this time of the night? Damn you nigga!" She said, then chuckled.

Logik looked at her strangely.

"Fuck is you talking 'bout? You live in the ghetto. Don't even front like you don't see all that trash rolling down your block." He sarcastically reminded her.

Jazmine lived on the East Side, and in one of the wildest neighborhoods in the city. She started rubbing her sexy light-skinned thighs, as the effect of the Purple Haze started to kick-in. "True dat," she agreed, "well, all I got in there is some Frosted Flakes and Cinnamon Toast Crunch."

"Hell yeah! Go hook me up with that Cinnamon Toast Crunch. That's my shit right there." Champagne happily complied and went into the kitchen.

Logik watched her ass sway from side to side as she walked into the kitchen. *Damn Shorty, thick as hell!* He thought to himself.

An hour later, he was parking the Explorer back in front of Black's father's house. He got out and hopped into his Lexus. He stuck the key into the ignition as his cell phone started to ring.

Seeing that it was Jazmine, he answered it on the second ring.

"Hello."

"Well, hey to you too. I guess you was too busy to call and check up on your wifey all day, huh?"

"Yo, you already know what I got going on out here, Jazmine. So don't start that shit right here."

"I'm not trying to start anything with you. But we done had this talk several times before, and you agreed that you would at least call and check up on me throughout your day and let me know that you okay. I mean, I give you plenty of space to do you, Logik. I don't complain about a whole lot and I really don't ask much from you."

"Even though I don't fully approve of the lifestyle you live, I still accept it and love you no less. And to be honest with you, Logik. You still haven't earned my 100% trust back in your ass yet. Most women would've probably been left their nigga alone if they had physically caught his ass cheating on them liked I caught you, but I'm still here!"

She wiped a tear that escaped her eye and continued, "It's two o'clock in the fucking morning, and you ain't thought call me all fucking day! For all I know, you could've been dead, in jail, or anything!"

She started crying. "I'm just so tired of you disrespecting me like this, man. I can't keep going through this bullshit with you, Jermaine." She vented, as she laid in bed listening to her Jagged Edge CD.

Logik knew he was in the wrong once again, that's why he let her vent. Plus, he was using that time to think of a legitimate story to explain his actions.

Jazmine was the best thing that happened to him since his mother died. She did not deserve the type of treatment he constantly dished out to her. He loved her with his whole heart and would have literally died for her if it ever came down to it. It always fucked him up whenever she cried or was in pain.

He really wanted to be the type of man that he knew she needed and deserved. But fucking other women was like a drug that he was strongly addicted to. But really, he was addicted to the way he was able to please a woman sexually. He loved seeing the look on a woman's face when he was nine inches deep inside of them. He had the skills to make most women cum repeatedly at will. And he always knew how to find and molest their G-spot with ease.

"Yeah, I know I should of —"

She cut him off.

"Where you been at?" She suspiciously asked, knowing deep inside that he had been with another woman. "And don't even try to lie because I ain't stupid!" That, Logik already knew.

"If you stop cutting me off and let me explain, I'll tell you." He replied, as he came to a traffic light.

She spazed out, "Fuck that! Matter of fact, where your ass at now?" She was now pacing the room back and forth.

"I'm on my way home, that's where I'm at. So, you gone and let me finish saying what —"

"Ain't no need for us to have this conversation twice, so save your lies for when your ass get here."

Her phone number started blinking on the screen of his phone, indicating she had already hung up.

"Good." Logik thought. That would give him more time to strategize.

Chapter 4

GREEN ACRES PARK (also known as The Gap) was on the north side of Charlotte. It was crowded with locals from the Northside that Saturday, who were observing a competitive basketball game from the sideline that was going on.

Big E and about twenty other dudes from the Northside were all chilling inside one of the gazebo areas in the park, discussing the incident his brother Lil' E had with Logik at Ms. Pat's house.

"So Lil' E, you telling me that Logik and some of his homies just pulled out on y'all for no reason?" He quizzically asked. Big E, knew that his younger brother was a hothead and loved starting shit with people. But at the end of the day, that was still his little brother. Big E knew Logik was a dopeboy such as himself, who was about his bread. He just didn't see Logik starting some dumb shit for nothing when he knew that having a beef could be dangerous to himself and his hustle.

"Hell yeah, that's what happened!" Lil' E lied.

Big E looked at Jason. "You was out there too, right, Jason?" Jason was the one who had pulled his gun out on Black and Banks when they came to aid and assist Logik.

"Yeah, I been out there." Jason replied.

"So, is that what happened?" Big E asked suspiciously.

Jason looked at Lil' E, then back to Big E before he answered.

"Yeah, that's how it went down." Jason co-signed.

Big E started pacing with his hand behind his back, plotting his next move. Big E was like the Big Homey on the North Side. His word carried much weight on that side of town.

"A'ight, fuck it," Be E said as he clasped his hands together. "We gonna need about three unknown cars for what we 'bout to do."

"Yo, Krazy."

"What's good, big bruh?" Krazy anxiously replied.

"Make sure you get them three cars we need. We gone hit Ms. Pat's house and two other spots that them niggaz be at on the South Side at the same damn time."

"Shit, that's aleady done my nigga." Krazy assured.

LIL' E HAD a call he needed to make, so he left everybody under the gazebo and headed to his car for some privacy. As soon as he got inside the car, he pulled out his phone and scrolled down his contact list until he saw the person's name he wanted to call.

"What's up, Boo?"

Lil' E wrinkled his nose.

"Don't what's up me, bitch. Why every time I call your ass it seem like you keep sending me to voicemail?" He angrily asked.

"Unt-unh. I done told you about talking to me like that, Lil' E. Now, calm your ass down and stop tripping." She said defensively.

"Ain't no tripping shit! Why you keep ignoring my muthafucking phone calls, yo?" He seethed.

She cocked her head to the side on the other end of the phone, clearly irritated. She was getting tired of hearing him bitch.

"Look, I'm getting real tired of you disrespecting me, Lil' E. You gone make me cut your young ass off got-dammit!" This was the main reason she hated dealing with younger dudes. *Give these lil' niggaz a shot of some good pussy and they act a damn fool.* She thought to herself.

"Yo, calm down girl." The tone in his voice suddenly changed. "I'm just saying though, Champagne. I been hitting your ass up since yesterday. You told me to never pop up at your house unannounced, so I been calling because I been trying to come through." He explained, hoping he hadn't talked himself out of some pussy.

Champagne was an older chick who Lil' E met five months ago at Platinum City. Never in his young life had he experienced a shot of pussy as good as Champagne's.

He also felt that by having a thoroughbred bitch like Champagne on his arm would've boosted his popularity in the hood. But in reality,

Champagne was a well-known stripper throughout the city, and Lil' E was like the two-hundredth nigga to sample that pussy.

The boy was plain old pussy whipped.

One night when he was at her house, he went through her phone and checked her text messages while she was in the shower. He saw that her and Logik had been texting each other back and forth throughout that day.

In his mind, Logik was the reason that Champagne never wanted to settle down with him for. The type of texts he saw that Champagne had sent Logik were words that she never sent to *him*. He could tell by the texts that she was really feeling Logik, and this was the reason that Lil' E secretly hated Logik for.

"Whatever, nigga. Look, I'm at the house now, so if you trying to come through, you need to come on because I'm about to get my hair done for work tonight." Champagne said, knowing that she needed to give Lil' E some pussy to calm his ass down. The last time she gave him a dose of her medicine was a little over two weeks ago.

A wide grin appeared on his face. "That's what's up Shorty. Yo, want me to bring some weed over or summin?"

"Nah, Boo. But a bitch broke as hell though." She ran game. The only reason she was fucking with Lil' E is because he was a young hustler that she could easily manipulate for money. All she had to do was give him a little pussy every once in a while.

Thirty minutes later, Lil' E was sitting in Champagne's living room. Lil' E looked on hungrily as Champagne swayed voluptuously over to him. The only thing she had on was a long white t-shirt. She squatted down in front of him and unbuckled his pants.

He moved her hand. "You don't got to do all of that, Shorty. I'm just tryna fuck." He informed her, as he looked at her thick red thighs.

She put a finger to her lips silencing him. "Shhh. Let me do me." She commanded, moving his hand away.

She pulled his tiny dick out of his pants and swallowed it whole. The inside of her hot and wet mouth had felt like the inside of her pussy to him. Seeing her bob her head up and down on his dick sent him into a trance.

He tried to push her head off of his dick, but she pushed his hand out of the way. Moments later, he released his load deep down her throat. She swallowed and sucked him until she milked him dry.

"Damn, your head game official, Champagne. Super Head ain't got shit on you." Lil' E said panting, like he just got finished running a race.

Champagne wiped the saliva from her mouth.

"Lil' E, I need a favor Boo."

THE ONLY SOUNDS in the car were the metallic ratchets of cocking automatic weapons, as Big E, Face, and Pac-Man loaded their weapons.

The driver made a right turn on Ms. Pat's block. It was around nine o'clock at night and kids were playing and hanging around on the block like it was the Fourth of July. A little boy and his friends were playing basketball in the middle of the street on a crate that was nailed to a wooden light pole. The little boy was bouncing the basketball as he stared at the men with black bandanas on their faces inside of a dark-blue Chevy Caprice as it passed by. Being that the little boy was in the middle of showing his friends that he was "Lebron James," he thought nothing of the face-masked men in the passing car.

Both of Ms. Pat's grandsons, JuJu and Tyreek were sitting in her front yard, smoking weed and listening to the rap music that was bumping low from one of their friend's car that was parked in the front yard.

Tyreek was the first one to notice the assault rifle coming out the back window of the car.

"Watch out, gun!" He yelled, snatching JuJu to the ground right before automatic gunfire erupted and whizzed over their heads.

POW, POW, POW, POW, POW!

Tyreek, JuJu and their three homeboys scrambled to the backyard, as another burst of automatic gunfire from Big E's Calico blazed the front yard, blowing chunks out of the porch and door frame. Tyreek's homeboy Derrick quickly pulled his gun out starting firing shots at the car as he backpedaled toward the backyard.

Pac-Man hopped out the passenger-side of the car with a Mossberg in hand.

BOOM! click-clack-BOOM! click-clack-BOOM!

He worked the side action quickly on the Mossberg pump, releasing shots in rapid succession. He caught Derrick twice in the chest, send him flying backwards.

Tyreek and JuJu managed to take cover behind Ms. Pat's Ford Mercury and return fire. The pressure caused Pac-Man to jump back into the car. The driver of the Caprice then skidded off.

Melvin laid on the ground, chest heaving as he struggled to breathe. Ms. Pat's grandsons and both of their homeboys walked over and stood over Melvin.

"Aw, shit! They hit my nigga, Mel!" Ju Ju shouted as he kneeled down and held Melvin in his arms.

Melvin saw the lights approaching, then everything faded to black. He died with his mouth and eyes wide open.

Meanwhile, a couple of blocks over, a group of South Siders were standing in front of the corner bodega, smoking weed and serving local crackheads as they walked up. The screech of tires made them all turn their heads to the left simultaneously. Before they even had a chance to draw their weapons, the shooters were already jumping out of the black Chevy Tahoe with guns in hand.

"Sup, mufuckas!" One of the shooters hollered, as he took aim and fired relentlessly at the group of dudes in front of the bodega. He managed to drop Banks and a short dude with dreads instantly. His partner caught a heavy-set dude with dreads twice in his ass and once in the leg. The remaining two dudes made it inside the store in the nick of time, seconds short of missing death.

The two shooters pedaled backwards towards the Tahoe and quickly hopped in. Seconds later, the Tahoe disappeared into the night.

Lil' E, Jason, and Krazy spotted Sergio walking to his Acura, which was parked on Belview Avenue. Sergio was a well-known South Side representative who the North Siders had problems with in the past before the beef died down. Krazy had never liked Sergio. Now he had the motive and opportunity to finally put Sergio out of his misery.

"That's our man right there," Krazy said, pointing to Sergio who was walking to his car. "Yo Jason, hurry up and catch that muthafucka before he hop in his car!" Krazy ordered. The car leaped forward after Jason floored the gas pedal.

The only thing that was on Sergio's mind at the moment was getting home, taking a hot shower, and heading over to Platinum City. He was on the block all day and was physically and mentally drained.

As soon as he grabbed the door handle, a white Oldsmobile skidded to a stop beside him. By the time he turned around, it was too late.

BOC! BOC! BOC! BOC!

The four shots from Krazy's nine-millimeter brought Sergio's life to an end.

The wailing of sirens could be heard from a few blocks over, as three police cruisers headed to Ms. Pat's house, unaware of the third shooting that had just taken place.

Chapter 5

LOGIK SAT BEHIND the steering wheel of his Lexus listening to Anthony Hamilton. He and Jazmine were on their way back from her mother's house. Her mother had asked Logik a week ago, could be paint the guestroom in her house. He told her "yes," but seemed to never have the time to do it. Being that he was in the doghouse with Jazmine "once again," Logik had been over to her mother's house all that afternoon painting the guestroom. His way of trying to get back in good graces with Jazmine.

Logik had his phone turned off. He was already in the "doghouse," so he didn't need one of his freaks to call his phone while he was around Jazmine.

Jazmine's cell phone rang.

"Hello?"

"Yo, Jazmine," Black sounded out of breath. "Is Logik around you?"

She sensed the urgency in his voice and immediately became worried.

"Yeah, he right here Black. Hold on a second." She passed Logik her phone.

"What's poppin'?"

"Yo, I been tryna call your ass all day. What, you had your phone off or summin?" Black asked, but he didn't wait on him to reply. "Fuck all that though. Yo, somebody just shot Banks in front of the spanish spot on Manchester, dog!"

Logik pressed the phone closer to his ear, hoping that he heard Black wrong.

"What the fuck you just said, nigga?" He was angrily surprised.

Jazmine looked at Logik with worried eyes.

"Look, bruh. I'm on my way to Charlotte's memorial right now. Where you at?" Black asked.

"I'm on the interstate right now, but I'll be there in 15 minutes. Yo, let me get off this pho —"

"Hold on a minute dog, I ain't finished."

Logik put his left signal on before he crossed over into the far lane and blew past the other motorists.

"That lil' freak, Amanda, hit me up and said that a bunch of cops over there at Ms. Pat's house too and that it looked like somebody was laying on the ground dead. Now you know what all this shit looking like, right? Black asked.

Logik clenched his jaw. "Yeah, it look like them niggaz on the North Side better start investing in some muthafucking caskets." Logik replied with venom in his voice. "Yo, let me focus on driving right now, homey. We'll talk once I get to the hospital. One." He ended the call and handed Jazmine her phone back.

"Babe, is everything okay?" She quizzically asked, but already knowing something serious happened.

"Nah, yo, shit just got real." Logik said, more to himself than to her. Jazmine wanted to inquire more about the situation but chose to remain silent the rest of the ride. She also wanted to ask Logik why he had his phone turned off, but that would have to wait, for now.

Logik turned his phone on and tried calling Ms. Pat and her grandsons, JuJu and Tyreek, but neither one of them answered.

THE EMERGENCY ROOM was packed as family and friends waited on the status of their loved ones. As soon as Logik and Jazmine walked through the automatic double doors, they spotted Black sitting with Banks' family so they walked over. Logik gave everybody a hug, then he and Black stepped off to the side, leaving Jazmine with Banks' family.

"Yo, what these doctors saying up in here about my nigga, Black?"

Black dropped his head and slowly shook it.

"Shit don't look good, dog. He lost a lot of blood and the doctor said some shit 'bout one of his lungs collapsing and whatnot." Water started to build up in Black's eyes.

Logik shook his head and tightened his lips to control is emotions. Then his phone started to vibrate.

"This JuJu right here." He told Black when he looked at his phone. "Hello?"

"Yo, big bro, them niggaz from the North Side shot my muthafucking grandmother's house up and kilt my homeboy, dog! Them niggaz almost killed me and my brother too!" He spazed out. "We 'bout to go over there and pop off on them fools now!" JuJu barked menacingly.

"JuJu, listen to me. I know shit crazy right now, trust me. Banks laying up in the hospital right now, fighting for his life, and I'm ready to pop off my damn self. But them streets hot right now lil' bro. Plus, them niggaz would be expecting us to retaliate right now anyway. So either way it go, going over there on the North Side right now would be the dumbest shit ever. Trust me on this."

JuJu sniffed. "Yeah, I hear you talking Logik, but we all out here right now ready to go to war!" He replied with authority.

"Listen, JuJu. Y'all niggaz fall back!" He noticed people started to look at him when yelled, so he lowered his voice. "Look, we gone see about them dudes real soon. Shit, just hot as —"

JuJu hung up on him.

Pissed off, Logik shoved the phone into his pocket.

"Fuck!" He said out loud.

"Wassup with JuJu?" Black asked after seeing Logik's reaction.

"Them hardheaded ass lil' niggaz 'bout to take their ass over there on the North and dumb out. Man, they gone fuck around and get their asses locked up or killed. Shit too hot right now." Logik stressed, as he looked around, making sure he wasn't talking too loud.

"Them lil' muthafuckas should know better than —."

"Oh, God no! Not my baby, Lord!" Banks' mother sobbed loudly after the doctor informed her that Banks didn't make it.

Immediately, Jazmine looked over at Logik after she saw Banks' mother's reaction. Logik was walking in circles with his hands clasped behind his head and tears running down his face. Jazmine went over to comfort her man. She grabbed Logik and hugged him tightly, allowing him to cry on her shoulder.

JUJU DID NOT take heed to the advice that was given to him. As soon as he hung up the phone with Logik, he and his brother Tyreek, and several of their homeboys loaded into a mini-van and headed to the North Side.

A passing police cruiser noticed a van full of suspicious African-American males, so he made a u-turn and threw on the blue lights.

"Ya'll think I need to pull over or what?" Tyreek nervously asked from the driver's seat, as he glanced at the five-o in his rearview mirror.

"Fuck that! We got too much guns up in here. Press the gas on that pig, Tyreek!" JuJu ordered.

Tyreek complied and sped off. His adrenaline was pumping so hard he could hear his heart beating in his ears. He made a lot of sharp and dangerous turns trying to lose the police cruiser behind him, but the van was just too slow.

The officer in the cruiser immediately radioed in for backup when the van failed to stop. He kept a safe distance behind the van as the driver drove recklessly throughout the city.

Tyreek attempted to make another sharp turn and lost control of the van. The van flipped over three times before it landed on its side and skidded to a stop.

Moments later, the van was surrounded by a bunch of white police officers who were itching to claim the life of another African-American.

Chapter 6

ONE O'CLOCK in the morning, Ms. Pat was sitting at her kitchen table with her brothers and two of her friends, smoking a Kool cigarette, and talking about the madness that happened in her yard earlier that evening. Law enforcement officers had finished up their investigation for the day at her house an hour prior.

Monique came walking into the kitchen from outside, where she had just finished smoking a $20 piece of crack rock. She went to the refrigerator in search of a beer when the cordless phone on the kitchen wall rang.

"I'll get it Ma." Monique said as she grabbed a beer and closed the refrigerator door.

"Hello? Yeah, she right here, who's speaking? Hold on a minute."

"Ma." She said, handing Ms. Pat the phone.

Ms. Pat blew a cloud of smoke out of her mouth before she spoke, "Yes?"

"How you doing, Ms. Pat. My name is Roshelle, I'm your grandson JuJu's friend. I used to call your house for him in the past and I still had your number stored into my —."

Ms. Pat was ready for the girl to get to her point.

"Spare me the details, honey. It's a lot going on right now and I hope you can just get to what it is you're calling me for."

The girl rolled her eyes on the other end of the phone.

"Yes ma'am. Well, I was just riding down Washington Boulevard and I saw the police had both of your grandsons and some of their friends on their knees in handcuffs. It looked like your grandson and them wrecked the van that they was in, too. I just called because I thought that you might want to know about your grandsons."

"Well, I sure appreciate you caring enough to call and inform me about that, babe." She smashed the cigarette out in her ashtray. "Where was they at on Washington Boulevard, Roshelle?"

"Oh, they in front of the McDonald's by the mall, ma'am."

"Are they still out there, honey?"

"Yes, ma'am. I just passed them less than five minutes ago."

"Thank you so much for calling me sweety. I got to go now." She hung up quickly, leaving Roshelle looking dumbfounded on the other end of the phone.

"Stank bitch." Roshelle barked into the phone after Ms. Pat hung up.

Ms. Pat told her brothers, Gerald and Earl what Roshelle had just told her concerning JuJu and Tyreek. She wasted no time grabbing her purse and the keys to her Lincoln Town Car, then her and Earl headed for Washington Boulevard, leaving Gerald with her friends.

The red, white, and blue lights from the EMS and police cruisers lit the area up like a disco ball. Ms. Pat parked the Lincoln in the McDonald's parking lot, then she and Earl walked toward the scene of the accident. She noticed two EMS workers loading up a young black man on a stretcher into one of the ambulances.

As they were heading towards the EMS, a loud thumping sound startled them. When they turned their heads towards the noise, they saw JuJu in back of one of the police cars beating on the window trying to get their attention. They changed direction and started walking towards JuJu. She noticed three officers talking amongst each other and pointing at JuJu, so she and Earl approached them first.

"Excuse me, can someone tell me what's going on here?" She pointed to Ju Ju in the back seat of the police car. "That's one of my grandsons right there."

A white pale-skinned officer spoke for the trio. "Yes ma'am. Well, as of now your grandson is about to take a ride to the station for questioning and possibly charged with a crime. Also, one of your grandson's friends aimed his gun at several officers and was shot several times. If you —."

Ms. Pat's heart skipped a beat when she heard that.

"Who was shot? W-what's the name of the other boy that was shot? I think my other grandson is out here too." Ms. Pat was a nervous wreck.

"What's your other grandson's name ma'am?

"His name is Tyreek Galloway." She told him.

The pale-faced officer looked at the other officers standing next to him, puzzled.

The black, chubby male officer replied, "No ma'am. He wasn't the individual that was shot, but he is another individual that's going to be taking a ride to the station for questioning. There were several firearms found in the vehicle your grandsons were in. We should be wrapping things up here real soon, but you are more than welcome to come down to the station when we're done here."

Chief Frederick Jackson was talking to one of the deputies at the time. He saw Ms. Pat and Earl talking to his officers, so he excused himself and headed in their direction.

"Excuse me, gentlemen." The Chief said when he walked up. "Ma'am would you like to step over here a minute?"

Ms. Pat, Earl, and the Chief stepped off to the side.

"How are you doing Patricia?" He spoke to Ms. Pat first, referring to her by her first name. "What you say, Earl?" He extended his hand to Earl.

"I'm alright, Chief. Me and my sister just trying to get some understanding on what happened with my nephews out here." Earl explained.

"Well, I'm not going to beat around the bush with you Patricia. Your nephews was riding in that van over there." He pointed to the overturned van.

"The driver of that van led my officers on a high-speed chase before he lost control of the vehicle. When my officers surrounded the van, one of your nephew's friends was spotted holding a gun which he refused to let go of, and which eventually led to him being shot. Now, the good thing about that is that the young man will survive his injuries."

He paused, then looked at Ms. Pat.

"A young man was just killed in your front yard several hours ago. Not to mention two other shootings that happened around the same time that the shooting at your house happened, Patricia. And all of these shootings happened in the South Side area. Now, here we have your grandsons and some of their friends riding in a van with several guns in it, and the driver of that van led one officer on a high-speed chase before he lost control of the van." Chief Jackson scratched his head. "You kind of see how all of this is adding up Patricia?"

Ms. Pat sucked her teeth.

"This whole story you just put together would sound real good in court, I'm sure. But, majority of what you saying could all be a coincidence as well, Frederick. They all are innocent until proven guilty, you know?" She reasoned, defending her grandbabies.

"Look, I'm just pulling your coat to all the information I've gathered thus far. It's a strong possibility that we probably saved your grandsons lives or maybe the lives of some others tonight."

Ms. Pat couldn't argue with that.

"Earl, excuse me and the Chief for a minute." She told Earl, as her and the Chief walked off.

"Listen Fred. We've known each other for a long time and I understand that you got a job to do and everything, but these are my grandbabies we're talking about. Now, I don't know what all you can guarantee me concerning them and whatnot, but as a favor from an old friend, I need you to find a way to keep my grandsons from going to jail. Now, if they get their black asses in something else later on down the line, then I would expect that you would have to do what you would have to do, and I won't fault you for that. But for this time, as a personal favor, I'm asking for your help Fred."

He thought for a few seconds.

"Patricia, look. They're going to run prints on those guns. There is absolutely nothing I can do about that. If the driver or the owner of that vehicle don't claim ownership of those guns, then each of them will get charged. There is nothing I can do about that either. Now, tomorrow the Mayor is going to be calling me and wanting some answers for everything that took place in her city in these last couple hours. But if it comes down to it that your grandsons might have to sit in the county jail until they can get a bail set for them, then it's nothing I can do about any of this Patricia. Other than speak with the judge before the hearing and ask him to grant your grandsons a lower bail." He shrugged his shoulders. "But, that's all I can do to help out this time Patricia."

Ms. Pat nodded her head understandingly.

THE INSIDE OF A.M.E. Church of Christ was packed to capacity. People were lined up against the walls because there was no room in the pews. It seemed as if the whole city came out to pay their respects to Desmond "Banks" Wallace.

Logik and Jazmine sat in the fourth pew behind Banks' family as they listened to Pastor Bailey give the eulogy from the pulpit.

"....for man also does not know his time. Like fish taken in a cruel net. Like birds caught in a snare. So the sons of men are snared in an evil time, when it falls suddenly upon them." Pastor Bailey closed his bible after he read the scripture. He was reading from Ecclesiastes, Chapter 9, Verse 12 out of his New King James Bible.

Jazmine leaned over and whispered in Logik's ear. "You alright babe?"

He clenched his jaw and nodded his head, unable to take his eyes off the pearl-white casket in front of the pulpit which held his comrade.

The pastor continued, "Children are suppose to bury their parents. Parents are not suppose to bury their children...that's how life suppose to work, you see. Your parents take care of you in your younger life, then you take care of your parents in their older life." He wiped his brow with his rag. "So in reality, we all are put here to live and help others to live. That's how the cycle of living was meant to work. We live to let live....it's not normal when a parent has to bury their child before their child was able to truly live and partake in this cycle of life.

He paused.

"That's not normal, and we must program that into our minds until that becomes our reality!" He wiped his brow again, "It's not right when a mother or father has to bury a child of theirs who died by the hands of another man." He pointed to the casket. "Gunned down in the streets like an animal!"

A few sniffs could be heard throughout the church.

"Gunned down in the street by someone who look just like him. Gunned down in the street by someone who was going through the same everyday struggle as him! That's not normal!" Pastor Bailey emotionally preached, causing Banks' mother, Ms. Wallace to cry hysterically. Her daughter and Banks' baby's mother wrapped their arms around Ms. Wallace, then the trio slowly rocked from side to side in an attempt to comfort each other.

Seeing Banks' three favorite women so emotionally torn apart caused a stream of tears to run down Logik's cheeks. He was staring at the pearl casket menacingly, with thoughts of punishing the people that were responsible for ending his comrade's life.

BANKS' MOTHER HAD a "sitting up" that night at her house. Banks' sister Felicia and two of his aunts were in the crowded kitchen preparing plates for those of the guests who wanted to eat. Ms. Wallace's yard was packed with family and friends, and cars were parked on both sides of the street.

In the backyard of Ms. Wallace's house, a hushed meeting was taking place between a group of South Siders.

Everyone had on dress clothes, most were packing heat, and everyone wore a serious-looking face.

"Listen man. A lot of shit is going on right now. Ms. Pat's grandsons locked up. The South Side lost four good niggaz to them North Side bitches. The pigs got the streets hot, and we just got finish laying to rest another one of our peoples today. We all fucked up about everything that's going on, and our trigger fingers are itching to bring about justice."

Logik sighed.

Ya'll think I ain't ready to make some niggaz bleed?" Logik barked. "That was my right hand man who body I helped carry out today. But we still need to fall back until some of this heat die down. Each step gotta be calculated. The only priority in war is winning the muthafucka."

Black interjected.

"I ain't feeling all this waiting shit, Logik. We been waiting almost a fucking week now. I understood why we fell back that night the shit went down, and a few days after that. But, now you telling us we need to fall back some more?"

Black shook his head. "Nah, I ain't feeling that shit homey. I say we go see them niggaz tomorrow. Banks was the last one of our people that got laid to rest today, so we gone fall back and respect this day. But tomorrow we riding on fools. That's what I'm talking 'bout!" Black aggressively protested, drawing a few "head nods" and "true dats" from several people.

"We gone get all them niggaz, that ain't even a second thought. But if we can get at these niggaz with less casualties, and less money we have to spend towards bonding muthafuckas out of jail or hiring lawyers. Then that's the best way to go about that shit."

Black took a swig of the Hennessy and then wiped his mouth with the back of his hand before he spoke. "And who made you The Don, nigga? We all our own man out here." Black smartly said. He was drunk on and on the verge of causing a disturbance like he always did whenever he was on the bottle.

Logik started getting real angry at Black. Even though he had a closer relationship with Banks than with anyone else out there. He was still trying to handle the situation in a way that was best for all of them as a "whole"."

Black was drunk and speaking off of emotions rather than with common sense. Logik hated getting into dumbass debates with Black. Especially when he was under the influence. Logik stepped in front of Black and stood inches from his face.

"Yo, you talking reckless cuz you on your drunk shit right now, my nigga. But drunk or sober, if you disrespect me like that again homey, I'mma put my hands on you." Logik stated bitterly.

Logik then made eye contact with the whole group again.

"If we catch them niggaz with their pants down, then we'll do more damage. Like I said, we need to fall back on that a little while longer." Logik stated matter-of-factly.

Black took another swig of Hennessy, while he looked at Logik with a cold stare.

Chapter 7

THE NEXT DAY, Logik pulled into the parking lot of an abandoned building and parked next to a white Chrysler 300. Inside the Chrysler sat his cocaine supplier, Frank. Logik had brought eighty-four thousand dollars with him to purchase three bricks of coke from Frank.

He grabbed the small gym bag off of the passenger seat, got out, then hopped inside the Chrysler.

Frank turned in his seat to face Logik.

"Damn, playboy. Don't tell me them females got you looking like that?" Frank asked sarcastically, referring to the wrinkled clothes Logik had on. Frank was unaware of the effect the past week had had on Logik.

"Nah, man. I just got a lot going on right now."

"Well, whatever it is, I see it ain't stopped you from getting paid." Frank said, as Logik was pulling rubber band stacks of money out of the gym bag.

After he left Frank, he headed over to his cousin Melinda's house to drop off a brick to cook up for him. Melinda had learned how to cook up coke from her baby daddy who was now serving three hundred and twenty-four months in a federal prison.

When Logik left Melinda's house, he went and rented a room at the Holiday Inn so he could add cut to the other two bricks he had, then call his customers up to let them know he was back in business.

Three hours later, he was riding down Myrtle Avenue when his phone rang.

"Hello."

"Big bro, what's da bizness?"

"You. What it be like soldier?" Logik asked Marcus.

"Cooling. Yo, I got a word on them two muthafuckas that robbed me."

"Word."

"Yep. Me and Budda gonna have a three-point shoot-out with them later if the weather look right." Marcus spoke in codes, letting Logik know that he and Budda were going to go blast one of the dudes that robbed him if they were able to locate him.

If it ain't one thing it's another. Logik thought to himself.

"Where you at right now?" Logik asked.

"We at the trap, big bro." Marcus replied.

"A'ight. Ya'll hold tight, I'll be through in a few."

"Say no more."

"Peace."

"Peace, bruh."

As soon as Logik ended the call with Marcus. His phone rang again. The caller id showed that the number was marked "Private."

"Hello?"

"Logik, how you and fam?"

"Who this?"

This Smurf, homey."

Logik's eyebrow raised.

"What Smurf this is, and how did you get this number?"

"This Smurf from Hillside Gardens, bro. I had got your number from Bank before that bullshit happened to him."

What was crazy is that Banks was dead and Logik had no way to confirm whether Smurf was lying or not.

"Yeah, a'ight. So what's up then?"

"I'm tryna spend some bread wit'chu."

"Okay, what you talking 'bout?"

"I need 41/2." Smurf replied, referring to the 41/2 ounces of cocaine he wanted.

"Where you at?"

"I'm leaving Kingsbury Mall right now, but I can meet you wherever."

Logik never served Smurf before. He knew that Banks used to deal with Smurf like that, and he seriously doubted that Smurf was a jack boy. But to be on the safe side, Logik decided he would drop the rest of the work he had off at this Aunt Vanessa's house before he went to serve Smurf. That way, if Smurf was on some jack boy shit, he wouldn't get hit for everything.

Plus, he was strapped as well, so Logik decided to roll the dice on this one.

"Meet me at the Flying J in 30 minutes, and park somewhere by the entrance. What you driving?"

"I'm in a black Monte Carlo on some fours."

"A'ight, I'll be in a silver Lexus."

"No doubt."

LEAD NARCOTICS INVESTIGATOR Ted Conwell sat at the communications console with his headphones on, ready to listen to the truck's digital recording equipment record everything that their wired confidential informant transmitted back to the van.

Moments later, Logik's silver Lexus pulled into the Flying J truck stop.

"Okay gentlemen. Here we go." Detective Conwell said to the small group of officers inside the can with him. He was building a case against Logik and had no means on taking him down that day. Detective Conwell used a crackhead to get to Smurf. Now he was using Smurf to get to Logik, and he hoped that he would be able to use Logik to get Frank if Logik was willing to become a rat and set up Frank. Detective Conwell knew he would then have to get the Feds involved.

It was all about the bigger fish.

"Okay, Smurf. Just like we practiced. Get him to implicate himself as much as you can, you got that?" Detective Conwell bluntly asked Smurf through the transmitter.

Smurf cleared his throat. Feeling more like a sucker each time he did what he was about to do. "Yeah, I got you."

Logik found an available parking spot two spaces over from where Smurf was parked. As soon as he put his car into park, he tapped the horn lightly, signaling for Smurf to walk over.

Logik placed the .40 caliber on his lap, covered it with his t-shirt, then hit the unlock button on his doors when Smurf walked up.

Smurf got in.

"Wassup, my nigga." He extended his hand to Logik for a shake, which Logik ignored.

Logik had his left hand clutching the .40 caliber under his shirt. Smurf's vibe had Logik skeptical about serving him, but he had done come too far to listen to those feelings now.

"I charge thirty-nine for the big." Logik told Smurf, referring to the 41/2 ounces by its nickname, and letting Smurf know that he wanted thirty-nine hundred dollars for it.

Logik was watching him closely.

"I know it's a drought and everything Logik, but damn. Four and a half ounces of cocaine for thirty-nine hundred dollars kind of steep, bruh." The way Smurf said "cocaine" made Logik look at him strangely.

"That's the ticket on them, homeboy. You want 'em or not? I got other shit to do." Logik asked impatiently.

He was just ready to serve Smurf and bounce. Today would be his last time serving Smurf. The boy just made him too nervous.

Smurf didn't know if he had gotten Logik to say enough on the recorder for the DEA or not, and at that moment he didn't care. Logik's body language was making him feel some type of way. Not to mention how he noticed Logik clutching something under his shirt.

"Yeah, let me get it then, bruh." Smurf replied, reaching into his pocket for the money.

After they made the exchange, Smurf got out and walked back to his car.

Logik pulled out of the truck stop parking lot and merged into traffic, never noticing the brown van that was parked across the street.

Chapter 8

LOGIK PULLED UP in front of his young soldier's trap house and parked. Budda was on the side of the house serving a friend when Logik pulled up. As soon as he finished making the sale, he walked over to the Lexus.

Logik got out of his car.

"Sup, big bruh?" Spoke Budda, pumping fists with Logik.

"Peace. Where Marcus at?" Before Budda could reply, Marcus came walking out the front door with a blunt in his hand.

After Marcus gave Logik some dap, he reached into his back and pulled out a folded sheet of paper and handed it to Logik.

When Logik unfolded the paper, he noticed that it was a "Wanted" poster with a man's picture on it. The caption said that 38 year-old Alonzo James was wanted for armed robbery in connection with a gas station being held up.

"So, this one of them fools that got you, Marcus?" Asked Logik, as he continued to study Alonzo's face on the wanted poster.

"Yeah, that's one of 'em. That's the muthafucka who had the scar on his face." Replied Marcus with steel in his eyes. "I snatched that shit off of a light pole earlier. I asked a few friends on the block if they knew that nigga, right? Fuck round, crackhead Barbara said, 'Oh, that's crazy-ass Lonzo from Park Village.' So, me and Budda gonna slide over there tonight and see if we can find that muthafucka before five-o do."

Park Village was located on the Eastside.

Logik gave Marcus the poster back.

"A'ight, ya'll do that. Remember though, incognito my nigga. Be mindful that five-o probably gone be in that area looking for that nigga as well." He warned them, wanting his young soldiers to be on point.

"Yeah, we gone be on point, big bruh." Marcus assured.

SOON AS LOGIK left Marcus and Budda, he drove to AutoZone to buy some antifreeze and brake pads for his Lexus.

When he pulled into the parking lot of AutoZone he saw Patience getting out of her Honda Accord. He parked next to Patience (being that it was the closest available spot towards the entrance of the store.)

Patience had on a cream-colored skirt suit and a pair of brown pony skin stiletto boots on her feet. The skirt suit she wore looked as if it was spray painted on her Coca-Cola bottle shaped body.

When Patience saw Logik's Lexus pulling into the parking space, she stalled and pretended like she was searching in her purse for something.

Dayum Patience, looking gooda than a muthafucka, thought Logik when he saw her.

He put the car in park and got out.

"I know you ain't come out the house dressed like that just to come to AutoZone?" Sarcastically asked Logik with a smirk on his face.

Patience blushed. *He checking me out,* She thought to herself.

"Puh-leeze! I just got back from my sister's graduation." She truthfully replied. "My damn car keep acting all crazy. Every time I slow down for a light or for a stop sign, my car keep cutting off," explained Patience.

"Sound like it could be one of your sensors or summin?" He speculated. "But, go inside and let them know you want them to do a diagnostic on your car. I believe that do that shit here for free." He suggested.

"And that will let them know what's wrong with my car?"

Logik nodded his head, trying his damnedest not to stare at her figure.

"Oh, okay." Patience was trying to think of something that would keep Logik talking to her. "Look, I wanna tell you summin," she paused, and placed her hand on her hip, "You need to be more careful creeping, Boo Boo. Especially when you choose to creep with a big mouth bitch. You know that girl Kim, who used to talk to Banks' cousin Nate?" He nodded. "Well, I hope you know that she going around letting the whole world know that she give you some pussy," she paused, "but you ain't gotta worry 'bout me running my mouth to Jazmine." Patience shook her head. "I don't get down like that. Whut'chu do is your business...besides," she looked him up and down seductively, "what Jazmine don't know won't hurt her, right?"

Logik chuckled. He had caught on to Patience's flirtatiousness.

"Patience, you wild as hell, girl." He rubbed the side of his face, trying to not look at her curvaceous body. "Make sure you get them to do that diagnostic on your car, a'ight?" He reminded her before he walked off.

Puhleeze! I know you a dog. Jazmine know you a dog. And damn near every bitch in the city know you a dog, but you always ignoring me like I'm one of these two dollar ass bitches or summin! But you know what? Fuck you nigga! Patience said in her mind, what she really wanted to say to Logik at the time, but she kept her thoughts to herself and walked into the store.

Logik hadn't heard from his boy Black in two days. He knew that Black probably still felt some type of way about the dispute they had in Ms. Pat's backyard after the funeral. *This nigga know how I get down. He knew damn well that I'mma ride for my man. But nah, Black wanted niggaz to react off of emotions without thinking first. Anyway, let me call this fool and tell 'em to meet me on the block so I pull his coat to this plan I got laid out for them North Side fools this weekend.* Thought Logik, as he cruised down the street after leaving AutoZone.

He pulled out his phone and dialed Black's number. After it rang twice, the voicemail came on.

Yo, I know this nigga ain't ignoring my call? He quizzically asked himself. Usually if a person have their phone turned off when someone is trying to call them, the voicemail system would automatically come on before the phone even rang. But if somebody was purposely trying to ignore someone who was calling them. Then the phone would ring once or twice before the voicemail system came on.

He tried Black again and got the same results.

"Fuck dat nigga!" Logik said out loud ending the call.

Ms. Pat had spoken to Logik in the church's parking lot after Banks' funeral about some of the things her and Chief Jackson discussed. She told Logik how the Chief had suspicions the shootings were all related to a conflict between the North and South Side boys. She said the Chief stopped by her house the other day after her grandsons were arrested. The Chief told her to let her grandsons know that as soon as they get released from jail that the North and South side would be under heavy police surveillance for two weeks, and that it would be wise for her grandsons and his friends to keep a low profile.

So the plan Logik had was very simple. Find a way to get muthafuckers to fall back for at least two weeks until the heat died down, then retaliate. He couldn't just come straight out and let them know what the Chief had told Ms. Pat, because that would have betrayed her trust in him. So the coming weekend would be the perfect time for them to retaliate against the North Side boys, and not a day sooner.

Logik headed back to his aunt's house to retrieve some of the work he dropped off there earlier before he served Smurf. He had a couple of ounces he needed to serve several people, before he took his car to get serviced on.

LATER THAT NIGHT, Logik and Jazmine were riding down Fulton Avenue in Jasmine's Acura. They had just gotten finished eating dinner at the California Dreaming restaurant.

"Yo, when was the last time we got new tires for your car, Jaz?" He asked, as he drove her car. Nothing had seemed wrong with her tires. He was just asking out of curiosity.

"Umm, what you said babe?" Jazmine hadn't heard Logik's question. She was preoccupied on her phone on Facebook at the time. A girl Jazmine knew had just posted a comment about Jazmine on her page.

"I asked you when was –"

"Unt-unh! Bitch I know you didn't!" Her loud outburst had cut Logik off in mid-sentence. She had just got finished reading the disrespectful comment a girl on Facebook just posted about a picture Jazmine posted on her page of her and Logik.

He looked over at Jazmine.

"Who you talking to?" He quizzically asked.

"This stank-ass, bald-headed ass bitch got the nerve to post some bullshit on my page!" She fumed. "Ooh, when I catch that bitch, I'mma beat that ass!"

"Yo, I don't know why you be following up that Facebook drama. That's why I deleted my page."

She turned to face Logik. Looking at him coldly.

From the way Jazmine was looking at him, Logik already knew that whatever comment the girl had posted on Jazmine's page was pertaining to him.

"Nigga, I know you're lying ass still be cheating on me. This must be one of your little hoes who posted this bullshit on my page!" She angrily assumed, holding her phone up to his face for him to see as he drove.

He squinched his face up and looked at her.

"Fuck is you talking about?"

"I had wrote 'Me and My Boo' under a picture of us that I posted on my page, and this bitch," she gestured with her head towards the phone in her hand, "she posted a comment about our picture and say 'your Boo and everybody else's. lol'" Water started building up in Jazmine's eyes. "Did you fucked her too, huh!?"

"Who!"

"This bitch!" She replied, shoving the phone in his face so he could see the girl's profile picture.

He quickly studied the picture.

"Yo, who the fuck is this? I don't even know this girl!"

"Oh, now you don't know the bitch?"

"Look, Jaz. I don't know who the fuck that ugly ass girl is. She probably friends or summin with somebody I done cheated on you in the past with or summin, I don't know? I already told you I'm done with all that cheating shit, Boo. We done been through too much for you to let some petty shit like this ruin our night."

She sucked her teeth. "Whateva, nigga."

"Look Jaz. I don't even know that ugly ass girl. You already know bitches gone hate whenever they see you doing better than them. I done fucked up on you several times in the past and we done got past that. But that's the past, Ma. Look, we having a beautiful night and we don't need to spoil it behind some Facebook bullshit." He reasoned. "Go ahead and turn that phone off, Ma. And stop all that crying." He said as he rubbed the side of her face with the back of his hand.

Jazmine didn't know if the girl's comments had any truth to it or not. So she agreed to let the conversation drop and turned her phone off. They were on their way to the Comedy House to see Katt Williams.

She hoped that his jokes would make her feel better.

MARCUS AND BUDDA sat inside a burgundy Grand Am that was parked on the side of the Park Village housing complex. They gave a crackhead they knew $40 worth of crack to borrow his car. They had been parked on the side of the complex for two hours hoping to spot Alonzo.

"Fuck all this waiting shit, dog. We might as well get out and look for that nigga. I know he 'round here somewhere." Marcus said impatiently, gripping the fo-five in his lap.

"Nah bruh. Too many muthafuckas out here for that." Budda replied. He saw a lady with dingy clothes on speed-walking on the sidewalk towards the complex. "Po-po looking for this nigga too. If he out here somewhere, he probably inside one of them apartments or summin." Budda speculated as he pressed the button on the door, letting the passenger-side window down. "Look, I'm 'bout to send this crackhead bitch on a mission for that fool. Eh, yo!" Budda yelled as he stuck his head out the window, trying to get the dingy looking lady's attention. "Ehh, yo!"

The lady stopped dead in her tracks and snapped her head from side-to-side trying to locate the person who she assumed was calling her. She spotted Budda leaning out of the passenger's side window of the Grand Am waving her over. She then started speed-walking towards the car.

"Yo, hop in the backseat for a minute." Budda told her.

She bent down and looked in the car, trying to see if she recognized the two men. "And who the fuck y'all 'pose to be? I ain't never y'all asses 'round here before." She said with her eyes stretched wide open looking like a madwoman.

"Look, bitch. You tryna get high or what?" Asked Budda, as he juggled a few pieces of crack rocks in his hand.

She quickly hopped her stank-ass in the backseat of the car.

"Y'all looking for some action?" She asked as she licked her crusty lips, trying to make herself seem attractive.

"Action?" Budda turned his nose up. "Ain't nobody want action with your dusty looking ass." Replied Budda with disgust in his voice. He was looking at the lady like she had shit on her face.

"Yo, chill out bruh." Said Marcus. "Look, we looking for our uncle, Lonzo. You seen him around here somewhere?"

"And what ya'll gone give me for that information?" She inquired, as her wide-eyes looked at the crack rocks inside of Budda's hand. "How I know y'all even Alonzo's nephews?" For all I know, y'all could be the police."

Budda's face balded up. "We look like the muthafuckin' police to you, bitch?" He angrily inquired with venom in his voice.

Marcus nudged Budda's shoulder, "Yo, chill the fuck out!" he warned Budda. Marcus then faced the crackhead lady who's mouth kept twitching up because she was in a bad need of a hit. "Look, yo. We tryna find our uncle Lonzo. Now, if you tryna get these rocks, you need to help us out with that." Marcus bribed her.

"You talking about Lonzo with the scar on his face, right?"

He nodded his head. "Yeah."

"First off, how much crack y'alls gone give me? And I hope it ain't none of that bullshit these boys 'round here selling."

"We'll give you a fat fifty if you let us know where to find his ass at." Replied Marcus.

"Shit, that muthafucka at my house. He been up over there the past couple of days spending money and getting high as hell. His ass broke now, so y'alls can take his ass on for all I care." She nonchalantly replied as she dug in her nose.

Marcus and Budda looked at each other simultaneously, not believing how lucky they got.

"Yeah, cool." Marcus tapped Budda's leg. "Go head and hook her up, dog."

Budda shook his head. "Not until she show us how to get in her house and we make sure Unc' over there." He told Marcus.

She sighed.

"Man, I can just tell y'alls where I stay at." She suggested.

"Nah, yo. You gone take us to where you stay at. That's the only way you gettin' that dope." Said Budda.

She sucked her teeth. "Whateva, man." She pointed in front of them. "Drive to that stop sign right there and make a left." She directed with an attitude.

Marcus and Budda talked to each other in hushed tones the whole ride to her house.

Chapter 9

LOGIK WAS IN the shower, allowing the sizzling hot water to cascade down his entire body. Jazmine was standing in front of the bathroom's mirror, taking off her purple thong, getting ready to join him in the shower. Logik looked over at Jazmine, admiring her facial beauty and figure. She wasn't super thick, but her body was toned like a track star.

They both were tipsy from all the alcohol they consumed at the Comedy House. Logik was tired and had a lot of shit on his mind at the time, but Jazmine was horny and the only thing that was on her mind at the time was getting some dick from her man.

She grabbed a washcloth off the rack and stepped into the shower behind Logik. She started lathering her body up with her apple-scented body wash soap that was in the shower. Logik slightly slid over, allowing the mist to wash the soap off of her body. He took the washcloth out of her hand and started lathering her body up. Her nipples seemed to get harder from each one of his touches.

They stared into each other's eyes, then started kissing one another passionately. He then slipped two fingers inside of her pussy. "Mmm," she moaned out in pleasure as his fingers moved in and out of her slowly.

"Mmph!" He loudly moaned animalistically when she gripped his long, curved dick. He started kissing on her neck and squeezing her nipples at the same time. He then pushed her against the tiled wall, lifted her about 4 inches off of the shower floor and guided his rod inside of her wet pussy. He started grinding her pussy slowly with long deep thrusts. Jazmine's pussy felt like ecstasy to him. Logik had only gotten a couple of good strokes in before he had to pause. She was so wet and tight that he almost squirted prematurely. He was captivated by her beauty and the facial expressions she made as his dick slid in and out of her pussy with a slurping sound.

Logik could barely maintain his balance because his feet were slipping and sliding in the water as he made love to Jazmine against the shower wall.

They changed position.

Jazmine was now standing, bent over outside of the shower with both of her hands resting on the toilet seat. Logik had a firm grip on her ass as he pounded her pussy like a wildman."Oohh babe, ohhh shit, I'm cumming!" She cried out in pain and pleasure, as she bounced her heart-shaped ass against his lower stomach and creaming all over his dick.

He pulled out of her and stepped out of the tub. He stood in front of her looking down at her menacingly. Dick hard as a brick and sticking out like a spear.

The two mollies he popped before he left the Comedy House had him feeling like "Super Man."

Before they knew it, Logik and Jazmine were on the floor in the hallway making love. He pulled his dick out of her and then placed his head between her legs. He started sucking on her clit, while jabbing this tongue in and out of her pussy like a madman.

Her body started shivering like a bolt of lightning was passing through it as she reached her climax again. She started coming so hard, it looked as if she was pissing in Logik's face.

"Ooohh, this shit feel soo good, babe!" She yelled out in ecstasy. Loud enough to wake the dead.

He pulled his dripping wet face from between her legs. He threw both of her legs on his shoulders, before he rammed his dick into her gushing pussy hole. They half kissed, half devoured each other while still slamming their bodies together. She wrapped her legs around his waist like an elastic belt while Logik kept grunting and pumping like a wild animal. She knew he was about to climax by the way his growl was getting louder and louder. She looked at his face and saw that it had become grossly twisted.

"Aahh, fuck!" He pushed himself as deep as he could go and exploded deep inside of her. "Oohh, yes! Ahh, daddy!" She screamed out as she came with him.

To say he blessed Jazmine would be an understatement.

"Phew!" He exhaled.

Jazmine laid there with her chest heaving, damn near out of breath.

The molly still had Logik ready to go another round, but his mouth was dry as hell because the mollies had him thirstier than a butt-naked Arab stuck in the Arabian Desert.

He left Jazmine laying on the carpet in the hallway while he went into the kitchen to quench his thirst. He grabbed a gallon of spring water out of the refrigerator and drunk half of the gallon before he pulled it away from his mouth.

He walked back down the hallway to find Jazmine curled up on the floor fast asleep. Logik scooped her up and carried her into the bedroom. He placed her in the bed, then got in beside her.

He wasn't sleepy or tired at all, so he rolled a blunt, grabbed the remote control off of the nightstand, and surfed the channels. When he came across one of the news channels he paused when he noticed the news reporter standing in a familiar area.

She was reporting live from the North Side.

"This is Michelle Beard reporting live, Tim. I'm standing here on Shuler Street, which is located here in North Charlotte. About two hours ago, a deadly shootout took place right behind where I'm standing at." She pointed to the area behind her. "Two men were shot dead and four others were seriously wounded. Tonight, these three men are in police custody."

Logik immediately recognized all three of the men in the pictures when they appeared on his TV screen. Two of the dudes in the picture, he knew from the South Side, and the person in the third picture was his comrade Black.

"All three men were charged with double homicide, four counts of assault and battery with the intent to kill, among other charges. Investigators believe that the deadly shootings happened as a result of an ongoing feud which initially started almost two weeks ago, between individuals who live on the North Side and South Side areas of the city. Police are still on the scene investigating, and details are still coming in." The reporter announced. "Anyone with any additional information, we urge you to call the number to Crime Stoppers at the bottom of the screen. Tim, back to you."

"Thank you Michelle." The anchorman said, before moving on to the next story.

"Fuck." Logik angrily said in a low tone, not wanting to wake his sleeping beauty. *I told then dumb ass niggaz to fall back.* He thought to himself as he mean-mugged the television set.

He grabbed his cell phone off of the nightstand and dialed a number.

Chapter 10

AT NINE-THIRTY, sunlight shining through the window woke him. Logik assumed that Jazmine had already left for work because she wasn't in the bed next to him when he woke up.

He reached for the nightstand to grab his cell phone. He noticed that Jazmine had left him a letter next to it, so he grabbed the letter first and opened it up.

Dear Love,

First, let me say that last night was Amazing!! Some film director should've made a movie about our journey last night because I swear we had to be the first people that ever went to Jupiter. LOL. I'm serious though! By the way, my ass was sooo sore when I woke up this morning! And I'm still mad at your ass about making me hurt my knees and bruising my arm. I sooo did not feel like getting up when the alarm clock went off this morning. I must have kissed you on your cheek a thousand times before I left for work....changing subject now.

Please be careful out in them streets today Boo, okay? I wish one day you would listen to me and we move away from all this madness in the city. I'm ready to have your child and we live like a normal family for once. Now, I do understand some of the things you was saying about the "American Dream," and everything. But, I would rather live that "American Dream" with you instead of living a glamourous life without you. Anyway, (because I don't want to bore you with my preaching), let me go ahead and leave for work before Ms. Tallwater's daughter have a fit. I'm already 30 minutes late (thanks to you and that BIG ASS DICK of yours! LOL!) I love you endlessly, babe and I will see you later.

Forever yours,

Jazmine

P.S. I made some omelets this morning and I left three of them for you in the microwave. Enjoy!

Logik smiled as he folded the letter up and placed it back on the nightstand. He grabbed his cell phone and dialed the directory.

"Directory Assistance. City and State, please."

"Charlotte, North Carolina." Logik replied, wiping crust out the corner of his eye.

"Thank you. And how may I help you in Charlotte today sir?"

"I need the number to the County Jail on Industrial Road."

"One moment, please."

Soon as he got the number he ended the call, then called the jailhouse.

"Charlotte Detention Center, how may I help you?"

"Yes, I'm calling to see if y'all have a Dontae Peterson in custody there?"

The corrections officer typed his name into the computer, then said, "Yes, we do."

"When is visiting hours?"

"He can have visitors from ten-thirty to twelve noon today, sir."

"A'ight, 'preciate it." He said, then hung up.

Logik rolled out of bed then headed to the bathroom for a shower. After the shower, he got dressed. He stepped into a pair of dark blue Rocawear jeans, brown construction Tims, threw on a tall white "Stop Snitching" t-shirt, and a brown New York fitted hat that complemented his Tims. He decided to leave his jewels home that day.

He warmed the omelets up that were in the microwave and ate them on his way to the county jail.

AFTER HE WENT through the normal visitation procedures at the jail, he was escorted upstairs to a visiting booth where he waited on the Corrections Officer to bring out Black.

A few minutes passed before the C.O. escorted a shackled Black into the small visitation room. Black spotted Logik sitting on the other side of the glass in the visitor's booth, so he walked over and sat down in front of the glass.

Both men picked up the telephone receiver.

"What?" Black said as soon as he picked up the receiver.

Logik peeped the attitude in Black's voice and saw it all over his face.

"What you mean, *what*? I came here to holla at my dog." Logik replied, looking at Black with a confused look on his face.

Black flicked his nose with his thumb then said, "Yeah, whateva."

"Yo, nigga. I see you still on that dumb shit." Said Logik. I had saw yo muthafuckin face all over the news and shit, so I came down here to see what's going on wit'cho ass."

"Well, now you see. I'm locked up in jail in this tight-ass jumpsuit and charged with all type of shit because I'm accused of riding for my brother."

Logik clenched his jaw.

"Yo, I know what the fuck you tryna imply dog, but you got Logik fucked up homeboy. You already know my war report my nigga, and you know how I move. But I ain't even 'bout to talk all reckless up in here though...anyway, I'mma drop a couple stacks on y'all niggaz books to help out wit—"

Black cut him off.

"I'm good homeboy. I got enough bread to handle my bizness with. So you can take whateva it was you was gone put on my books and add it to Mouse and Twan's books." Replied Black, referring to the other two dudes that were locked up with him.

Logik shook his head at Black's stupidity. "You's a real character my nigga."

Black looked at Logik with a sinister grin.

"Yeah, whateva nigga. You done?"

"Hmmpf! Yeah, I'm done." Replied Logik before he stood up, threw the phone on the counter-top and walked out.

After he left, he went to the Post Office and purchased three money orders. He put three thousand dollars on each money order. If a person was to spend ten thousand dollars or more, they would have had to fill out some Federal forms. Something Logik was aware of and definitely wanted to avoid.

As soon as he left the Post Office, he went back to the jail to drop off the three money orders, which would go directly on Black, Mouse, and Twan's books, even though Black's unappreciative ass said he was good. Logik still felt obligated to support his friends.

Real soon, Black would be respecting Logik's gangsta again.

THE ARRIVAL OF the cocaine drought, along with all the drama that had been going on in the city caused a ghetto crime epidemic. The crime rate had reached an all-time high and the Mayor of Charlotte was pressuring Chief Jackson to cool things down.

Election time was only two months away.

If the Mayor thought that the Chief had the ability to prevent these next murders from happening, she had another thing coming.

Drained from the day's activities, Logik was sitting on his bed, putting on a pair of black Tims that matched the rest of his outfit. Jazmine was sitting up in the bed, deep into the action that was on The Real Housewives of Atlanta reality show that was on TV.

She knew Logik was getting ready to hit the streets, but she wasn't upset like she usually would be. Since Banks had died, Logik had been spending quality time with her, so she had no reason to complain about that, but she started to worry when she noticed how Logik was dressed in all black, with a black sweater cap on his head, and none of his jewelry on.

"Babe, where you going dressed like that? I thought you told me that you was done robbing people since you had got back on your feet?" She questioned, half joking, half seriously.

He wasn't in the mood for 21 questions, so he acted as if he hadn't heard her and walked into the bathroom to take a piss.

When he finished, he headed towards the door to leave out, but he stopped when he caught a glimpse of himself in the bathroom mirror.

He studied the face that stared back at him, wondering if he was looking into the eyes of a killer. Logik had witnessed people get killed in the streets before, and he even shot several people (who all somehow managed to survive), but he had never taken a life before. And he certainly wasn't afraid to.

He grabbed a black and red duffle bag out of the closet in his bedroom, then threw it over his shoulder.

"Jermaine." Said Jazmine soon as she saw the evil look on Logik's face when he walked out of the closet. "Jermaine!" She said again, this time with authority in her voice when he ignored her the first time and continued to walk towards the door.

He stopped in his tracks, turned around and looked into her beautiful face.

"Babe, tell me you ain't about to do what I think you about to do?" She asked. His silence and the look on his face told her his answer. "Babe, no!" She frantically said as she got out of the bed and went to her man.

She grabbed both of his hands and held them in hers as tears poured down her face.

"Please, babe don't *goo*. I don't wanna see you get hurt, babe." She sobbed, pleading for Logik to change his mind.

He put his hands on both of her shoulders and looked into her eyes.

"Look, Ma. You already know what time it is. Now stop all that crying babe and be strong for me. You know your nigga know how da move. I'mma be safe Ma."

"Please babe. I don't want you to *gooo*!" She pleaded, then started crying uncontrollably into his chest.

He held her in his arms, as he ran his fingers through her hair while she sobbed into his chest. Unbeknownst to him, she reached behind him and started squeezing the duffle bag that hung from his shoulders. She heard the clanging of metal and automatically knew what was on the inside of the bag.

Jazmine knew her man, and she also knew that when his mind was made up about something, there was nothing any man or woman could do to change it. So the only thing that was left for her to say was, "Jermaine, promise me you'll come back to me in one piece?"

"I promise." He vowed, while inhaling the Chanel No.5 perfume she had on.

THE HUMID, SALTY air blew through Logik's dreds as he whipped through the Carolina streets with the window half way down.

The North Side was already hot, but since Black, Twan, and Mouse blazed them North Side niggaz last week, the North Side was now hell-fire hot. Plus, niggaz wasn't wasn't dumb enough to be out on the blocks like sitting ducks anyway. So, when Logik heard about a "big" block party that was gonna be on the west side of town that Saturday. Logik felt that the opportunity had presented itself for him to ride on his enemies.

To ensure that the main people he wanted to get were present at the block party, Logik used Champagne to lure them there. Champagne had told Lil' E that her and a few of her friends were going to be at the block party, and that she wanted him to bring Big E and some of his friends out there to hang with them. She informed Lil' E that her friends did not want to hang out with none of his friends and for him not to bring them.

Lil' E jumped at the opportunity to floss with Champagne in public. So he told Champagne, "Don't worry, Shorty. We gone be out there." He assured.

A few days ago, Champagne told Logik about her and Lil' E's fling with each other. She regretted ever getting involved with Lil' E's young ass because now it seemed like she couldn't get rid of him. If she wasn't so greedy for money, she never would have hooked up with him in the first place. Lately, Lil' E was starting to become violent towards her and she was too scared to completely cut him off because he knew where she rest her head at.

Logik could've got at Lil' E's ass, but he also wanted to eliminate Big E and a few other niggaz who be around him on the North Side that had influence. With them out of the way, the vicious attacks from the North Side would eventually stop.

Earlier that day, Logik had thought about bringing some of his homeboys from the South Side along with him for the mission, but he decided against it when the thought of interrogation rooms and the possibility of snitching ass co-defendants entered his mind.

He was on his way to drop the Lexus off at a crackhead house he knew so he could use her gray Mustang for the mission instead of his car.

As soon as he dropped his car off and hopped into the Mustang, he dialed Champagne's number as he backed out of the driveway.

Champagne's cell phone vibrated on her hip. When she saw that it was Logik, she walked off from the group.

"Wassup, Boo?" She spoke cheerfully.

"What it is? You still out there with them niggaz, right?" He asked, getting straight to the point.

"Yeah, Boo. I just walked off from them."

"Who exactly is them? Come on Ma, give a nigga some details."

She turned around and looked at Big E and his crew. "Umm, Big E, Krazy, Hakim, two other dudes I don't know and his lame ass little brother, Lil' E." She reported.

"So it's six of them, right?"

"Yep."

Logik was approaching a red light so he slowed down. "A'ight, look. Y'all still posted by the Green Street stop sign?" He inquired.

"Yep. We all still right here."

"Word. Yo, you kept ya mouth close like I told you to I hope?"

She rolled her eyes on the other end of the phone.

"Duh! I ain't stupid you know." She sincerely replied.

"That's wassup, Ma. You know you still good for them ten stacks I got for you though?"

"Hmmpf! I betta be cuz you know I don't be getting involved wit' no bullshit like this." Lil' E started looking at her angrily, so she put one finger up letting him know to give her a minute. "Just text my phone before the shit go down some and my girls can step off somewhere."

"Chill, Ma. I already told you, I got'chu." He reminded her.

"Okay. But let me go cuz this punk ass nigga keep looking at me funny."

"No doubt, no doubt." Logik nodded, in between tokes on the blunt as he drove the speed limit towards his destination.

Chapter 11

THE THUNDEROUS BOOM of the deep bass notes resounded throughout the area from the DJ speakers. Logik was parked about a hundred yards from the actual block party behind a pickup trick, watching Big E and company through his binoculars.

It was about 6:30 that afternoon, and the sky was starting to turn dark-blue as nightfall approached. The block was semi-crowded, and partygoers were starting to leave by the minute.

Logik reached into the duffle bag and pulled out two black .45 calibers. Both guns were already loaded and had rounds in the chambers, ready for combat. He also had a TEC-9 in the bag with an extended clip for backup in case shit got too hecked for him. He had on a pair of black leather gloves, careful not to leave his fingerprints on anything.

Marcus and Budda told him a few days ago how they had caught up with Lonzo and put his light out permanently. They had proven to be real soldiers. Logik was now wishing he had brought them along with him because he was starting to doubt whether or not he was able to handle all six men by himself. Not to mention the possibility of all of them being strapped.

The element of surprise would be the only advantage Logik had over his foes.

Logik got out of the car, strapped the duffle bag across his shoulder, and bobbed up the street. He had the sweater cap pulled down over his brow to help conceal his identity. Even though he was dressed like an assassin, no one paid him any attention.

He stopped about 20 feet behind Big E and his crew and leaned against a light pole. He pulled out his cell phone and sent Champagne a quick text, letting her know, for her and her friends to get the fuck out of the way. After Champagne read the text, he saw her telling her friends something, then a minute later the four of them walked off.

"This block party shit getting kinda whack, yo." Big E told his crew. "When them hoes get back, I'mma let 'em know to follow us to the Marriot. I'm tryna fuck summin, real talk."

"Word," Hakim co-signed.

"Yo Lil' E. That shorty Champagne badda than a muthafucka! I don't know why, but it look like I done seen shorty ass somewhere before." Said Krazy, as he pulled on the hair under his chin.

"Nah, I know you don't know her." Lil' E assured, not wanted them to know that he was flossing with a stripper chick in public like she was wifey.

Big E scratched the side of his face. "I don't know, yo. Shorty do look that that –" He was cut off in mid-sentence when two bullets tore into his face. Killing him instantly.

BOC! BOC!

Logik had both arms extended, squeezing the triggers in rapid succession, as he ran towards his victims.

BOC! BOC! BOC! BOC! BOC! BOC! BOC!

He had hit Lil' E three times in the mid-section and Hakim caught two to the dome when he tried to duck. The onlookers on the block were watching the scene unfold before their eyes in horror, then they started scrambling to get the hell out of his way.

Krazy managed to pull out his gun and got off a shot that missed Logik, but caught an innocent bystander in the neck. Logik was focused and did not flinch when the bullet whizzed past his face. He aimed his gun at Krazy and filled his chest with lead. Krazy was left lying on his side, eyes still open in an expression of the final horror.

The duffle bag that was strapped across Logik's shoulder was starting to get in his way, so he dropped it on the ground and proceeded to chase the other two dudes. He figured the reason they ran was because they wasn't strapped or either death scared.

BOC! BOC! BOC!

Two of the bullets caught one of the dudes in the back.

"Aarrghh!" Dude yelped in pain as he collapsed to the pavement.

A few minutes would go by before he stopped wheezing.

BOC! BOC! BOC!

The last dude must had ran track in high school because Logik's speed was no match for him as the four bullets whizzed past him. Logik decided to stop chasing the track star and ran back to scoop the duffle bag up and head back to the Mustang.

The effects of all the cigarettes had begun to catch up with him as his chest started to burn and his pace slowed down. It seemed like it took a lifetime, but he finally reached the Mustang and hopped in.

Scuurrrrr!!! Logik pulled off with screeching tires as sirens were approaching.

ABOUT AN HOUR after he left the bloody block party, he waited in his Lexus for Champagne in a secluded area off of a frontage road. He was ready to pay Champagne for her service and head home.

Logik was starting to get impatient because Champagne had said she would be there in 15 minutes. But that was 37 minutes ago.

He picked up his phone about to call her again when he saw the headlights from a car in his rearview mirror.

It was Champagne.

She pulled up behind him and killed the lights.

"My bad for keeping you waiting, Boo," She said as he approached the driver's side of her car. She had her window down. "I had to get my nerves together before I jump on the road. That shit was too crazy, yo. Your ass look like Rambo out that bitch." She snickered, but really felt like shit on the inside for her involvement.

"You good though, right?" He asked nonchalantly.

"Yeah, I guess," she replied, unsure how she really felt.

"Look, you think your homegirls could tell you had summin to do with that shit?" He quizzically asked, trying to pick her brain.

"I doubt it," She slowly started shaking her head from side to side. "Dayum, yo. I'm starting to feel bad about helping you do something like that, Logik. What if them niggaz on the north side find out that I set the whole thing up?" Champagne was a nervous wreck.

Logik had both of his hands behind his back the whole time.

"Oh don't worry. I don't think you gonna have to worry about that at all." He replied, then brought his right arm up from behind his back.

BOC! BOC!

He shot her twice in the head point blank range.

BOC! BOC! BOC!

Three more shots entered her body after her body tilted over.

Logik said that he didn't want any co-defendants for that mission. And he meant that.

Chapter 12

LOOKING UP AT the sun shining so brightly in the sky, Jazmine blocked her eyes with the back of her hand as she walked out the front door of Prudential Realty. She had just gotten finished paying the first three months of rent and the deposit fee for her and Logik's new home in a gated community on the outskirts of the city.

After the "Block Party Massacre" (as the news called it), Logik told Jazmine to start packing their things because they were moving. Even though not many people knew where they rested their heads at, Logik still didn't want to chance jeopardizing Jazmine's safety. The way he had laid his murder game down in public was very disrespectful, and retaliation could be highly possible (despite Big E being absent from the scene).

Logik had sent chills up Jazmine's spine when he came home that night and told Jazmine to help him pack because they were moving. When Jazmine saw the news the next day and learned about the "Block Party Massacre," she suspected that Logik been involved somehow. She wanted to ask him why they had to move, but deep inside she already knew the answer to that. She was getting fed up with the rollercoaster living and sincerely hoped that Logik would change one day. She didn't know how much more of living that way she was able to handle.

After they left Prudential, Jazmine drove to the U-Haul company so they could rent a U-Haul to get their furniture and belongings out of storage and take it to their new house. Logik grabbed the CD case in her car and started flipping through it.

"Damn Jazmine. Where the rap shit at?" He asked while continuing flipping through her leather CD case. "Oh, here we go. What you know about that, Pac, girl?" He asked after he stumbled across the Makaveli, 7 Day Theory CD and took it out.

"Boy, you sound dumb. I like these new rappers and all, but Pac will always be my baby," She looked at Logik and pinched his cheek. "After you of course."

Logik chuckled. "Well, shid. I ain't got nothing to worry about then because homeboy dead." said Logik as he attempt to put the Makaveli CD in.

"Unt'uh, baby. I don't feel like hearing no rap right now Jermaine." 2 Pac was her dude and all, but she did not want to hear any type of music at the time that would remind her of violence.

He wrinkled his forehead, "Whuddd!" He shrugged his shoulders then shook his head. "Whatever." He started back searching through her CD case again.

When he came across the Miseducation of Lauryn Hill, he said, "Yooo, this my jam right here." He took the CD out and put it in her CD player. He searched the CD until he found the song he was looking for. A few seconds later, Lauryn Hill's beautiful voice filled the car as she sung about the sweetest thing she even known.

Logik pulled out a Swisher Sweet cigar and started dumping the cigar tobacco inside a brown paper bag. He then pulled out a plastic sandwich bag which was half full of weed, and proceeded to roll up a blunt of that "fiyah."

Jazmine had always loved the smell of weed. She had smoked weed in the past before with Logik, but she promised herself that she would never smoke again, because the last time she smoked, the weed had her paranoid as hell.

"Dayum, that shit smell good," she complimented, looking at the light-green hairy buds that were in the plastic sandwich bag that was in Logik's lap.

"Oh, this that fiyah right here," said Logik as he broke the buds up into the cigar paper. "You want some?" He looked over at her smiling, remembering how she acted the last time she smoked.

"Boy, hell, no! You do you. I'll just enjoy the smell of it," she quickly replied.

He chuckled. "Yeah, I know that's right. You remember how crazy yo ass been acting that last time?" He clowned her.

She clenched her right fist and playfully jumped at him like she was about to hit him. "Boy, shut up!"

An hour and a half later, they had the U-Haul backed up to their storage unit while they sorted through their belongings.

"I shoulda got Peanut to help us with some of this shit." Logik thought out loud, as he stacked two boxes on top of each other.

"Puhleeze! I don't want that boy knowing where we live at," she said seriously. She never understood how Logik couldn't see the snake in his cousin.

But real soon, he would though. And by that time it would be too late.

"WHAT IT IS, Playboy?"

"Peace, bruh. How you?" Logik asked Frank.

Logik had hit Frank up for some work about two weeks ago but Frank was dry. The cocaine drought was severe and Frank told Logik that he would hit him up when he get situated.

He had texted Kenny the new number to one of his phones about a week ago, and he had been anxiously waiting to see Kenny's number pop up on his phone. Logik hadn't had any work in over two weeks and his pockets were starting to get thin. He had thought about robbing a dude name Quentin he knew. Quentin sold only weed and never seemed to run out of it. *I need to stick Quentin soft ass for some paper. Shid, that'll be a good 20 or 30 thousand dollars come up. Logik had figured, but then decided he would* be patient and wait on Frank to hit him up. He already had enough enemies.

He smiled when he saw Frank's number on the screen of his phone. "Everything good on my end. I just got back in town a few hours ago.

I'm over here chilling with my ladies now," Replied Frank, letting Logik know that he just got back in town, and that he had drugs on deck.

"That's wassup, Pimp. Shid, I'm tryna fuck at least three of them hoes," Logik spoke in codes, letting Frank know that he needed three birds.

"You know I don't save these hoes, Playboy," he paused. "Get with me in about forty-five minutes."

"No doubt."

"Later."

After Logik left Frank, he dropped off a brick to Melinda for her to cook up for him. Then he drove to the southeast side of town to drop some work off to Marcus and Budda. They had done blew most of their money and were ready to get back on their grind. Logik had sent a few texts out while he was at Melinda's house, letting his clientele know that the drought was finally over. His phone had been blowing up ever since.

It was about 10:15 pm and he was taking it in early. Logik had been grinding all day and he was exhausted.

He pulled into his driveway, got out, chirped the car alarm and walked into the house. Jazmine was sitting on the living room couch with one of her legs folded under her, watching the movie "Love and Basketball." She had her shoulder-length hair into a ponytail. The fairly new blonde highlights in her hair complimented her light skin.

"Hey, Babe!"

"Wassup, Ma?" He leaned over and kissed her on the lips. "Whut'cha in here watching?" He asked, as he turned around looked at the TV screen.

"Love and Basketball."

"I know you done saw that shit at least a hundred times already?"

"So! I love this movie right here. Especially the part where she played basketball against him for his love. Man I just love that," she replied as she placed her right hand on her chest.

"That's wassup," he said, then headed upstairs to take a shower. After the shower, he walked back downstairs and sat on the couch next to Jazmine. He wrapped his arm around her while sending Budda a text on his phone.

"Dayum! People don't know how to give you a break sometimes!" She angrily asked with jealousy in her voice.

"Keep running off at the mouth. You must want me to pop another one of them mollies again?" He jokingly asked, as he waiting on Budda to respond to his text.

"Mmm, you know I'm down for that." She replied, immediately becoming moist between her legs after he said that.

He chuckled, then his phone rang.

Jazmine cocked her head to the side and looked at him with the 'I know you ain't about to answer that' face.

"What it is?"

"Sup, big bro. Fuck you got going on?" JuJu asked. He, Tyreek, and a few more of his friends was chilling in Ms. Pat's front yard getting faded. He and JuJu had got out of jail two weeks ago.

"Ain't too much, in here chilling wit wifey," Logik replied.

"True dat," he said. "But yo, you know what tonight is right?"

"Nah," he replied in a very uninterested tone.

"It's my muthafucking birthday fool!"

"Oh, okay. Happy Birthday then."

"That's wassup, bruh. Look, though. We all going out tonight for my birthday. The whole South Side coming out to party with me!" He took a drag on the blunt he was smoking, then continued, "I know you over there chilling with wifey and whatnot, but damn bro. You must don't remember you gave me your word when you missed my birthday last year that you been gone fuck wit me this year? Damn, big bruh. Tell Jazmine I said take them handcuffs off your ass tonight!" Ju Ju joked.

Silence.

Damn! I did gave the lil nigga my word last year that I been gone fuck wit'em. But damn, why this fool birthday tonight? I know Jazmine 'bout to trip, but my word is my word...Fuck it! I need summin to get my mind off of Champagne ass anyway. I hate I had to merk Shorty, but I couldn't let her live knowing what she knew. I never shoulda never got her involved with that shit in the first place. All of these thoughts ran through Logik's mind as JuJu waited on his answer.

"What club ya'll going to?" Soon as heard the word "club" come out of Logik's mouth. She turned from the TV and faced him with a serious look on her face.

"Shiddd, you know we gone hit dat Moet tonight!" Excitedly replied JuJu, referring to Club Moet.

More Silence.

"A'ight then. I'll holla at 'chall when I get there."

"Word...Oh yeah, we gone be VIP too nigga."

"Yeah, a'ight."

"Peace."

Logik ended the call, but both of Jazmine's eyebrows raised in surprise.

"Unt'uh! This some bullshit Jermaine! You just got 'cho ass here, now you 'bout to leave back out?"

"Look, yo. I didn't knew it was JuJu's birthday tonight. I had forgot I had gave lil' bruh my word that I been gone fuck wit'em this year," Logik explained. He really didn't feel like spazing out on Jazmine's ass, but the look on her face told him that that was unavoidable.

Jazmine wasn't trying to hear that shit. She wanted to spend some time with her man that night. Plus, she was horny as hell and the dick was sitting right there next to her.

"Fuck that, Jermaine! I hate it when you always put me on the backburner for somebody else!" She exclaimed.

He had enough. "Look, yo! I'm a grown ass man, Jazmine. You talking to me like you got some muthafucking kids 'round this bitch or summin!"

"I ain't got none and damn sure ain't gone have none neither when you and that lil' ass dick of yours keep ripping and running down the damn streets all the time!" She yelled matching his tone. She knew that Logik's dick was far from being small, but she couldn't think of no other way to insult him at the time.

Little did both of them know, a little life was already developing inside of Jazmine's stomach.

Yo, fuck this. He said to himself before he got up and went upstairs to change, leaving Jazmine on the couch crying.

She wanted to apologize to him when he came back downstairs fully dressed and iced out, but her pride wouldn't let her.

He walked out the front door, slamming it behind him.

Chapter 13

THE SOUNDS OF OJ da Juiceman and Gucci Mane pumped loudly out the club's speakers when Logik pulled into the parking lot. A few of the club's security guards were in the parking lot with light sticks in their hands directing people where to park at.

Logik walked to the front of the long line, gave one of the bouncers a Benjamin, then disappeared into the club. He shook hands with several people he knew as he squeezed past party goers. He went to the bar because he wanted to buy the biggest bottle of Moet and Rosè that the club had, then head to the VIP section. As he stood there waiting on the beautiful dark-skinned bartender to return with the bottles of champagne he ordered, he saw Bank's sister, Felicia, sitting by herself at the end of the bar. She was saying something to some dude who it seemed she didn't want to be bothered with.

"...I'm saying though Shawty, you ain't gotta act like that towards a nigga. You should be glad I even came over here to holla at 'cho fat ass!" He bitterly told her.

Felicia wasn't obese fat, she was just a little on the plus size. She had a beautiful face and you could tell the way her body was shaped that if she was to ever lose about 70 pounds, her body would look like that of Mrs. Parker off of the movie 'Friday.'

Felicia looked at him with disgust, "Puhleeze, nigga! I know you ain't talking wit them raggedy ass teeth in your damn mouth. You ought to give me a tip just to look at your ugly ass!" She clowned him, unfazed by his comments of her.

"Fuck you bitch, you ain't all that anyway!"

"If that's the case, then why you brought yo ugly ass ova here for then?"

"Fuck you bit—" His sentence was cut short when someone placed a hand on his shoulder.

"Now, tell my sister you sorry nigga," Logik said menacingly as he stared at dude with steel in his eyes.

Dude was just about to talk shit, but it was something in Logik's eyes that was cold and threatening. Dude was only in the club with two of his friends and didn't know how many people Logik could've been in the club with. Plus, he wasn't even from the Queen City, he was from Atlanta and was several hours away from home. So it was either check this nigga with dangerous looking eyes, or apologize to the chubby girl who played him. He chose the latter.

Dude turned around and gave Felicia a fake smile. "My bad, Shawty," he said like the sucker he was.

"Yo, get the fuck out of here!" Logik stated, as he shoved dude away from the bar. Any other night, he would have just knocked dude's ass out for disrespecting his man's little sister like that, but he came to the club to have a good time and temporarily take his mind off of everything that happened in the past month.

"You a'ight, Felicia?" He asked putting his arm around her shoulders and sitting the two bottles on the bar.

She looked up at him and smiled, "Yeah, I'm straight. And thank you too."

"You already know. Yo, who you came out here wit?"

"I rode here wit one of my cousins." She could tell that he was about to ask her "which cousin," so she went on the say, "You don't know her though."

"That's what it is," Logik reached into his pocket. "You need some money or summin?" He asked her but was already peeling away a few bills off of his bankroll to give her.

"You don't gotta give me money everytime you see me, Jermaine." She said as she looked into his eyes. Felicia had always had a crush on Logik ever since she could remember. He had his dreds braided in cornrolls that night and Felicia thought that it make him look extra sexier.

"Oh ain't no thang. You know you my lil' shorty." He said as he wrapped his arm around her shoulders and pulled her into his chest in a brotherly manner.

Felicia's cousin had just came back from the restroom and walked up behind them. "Girlll, these niggaz up in here act like some wild animals." Felicia's cousin, Tabitha, told her soon as she walked up. "Hmmpf! Who's this, girl?" She asked referring to Logik as she looked him up and down flirtatiously.

"This one of my brother's friends right here...My bad, this was my brother's best friend right here," she corrected herself. "Logik, this is my crazy ba-hine cousin, Tabitha."

He nod his head at her, "Wassup, Ma?"

"You," she replied, then bit her bottom lip. Just looking at the boy got her pussy wet.

He turned his attention back to Felicia. "Yo, let me go so I can go get wit these fools up in VIP."

"Okay, thanks for the money too."

"No problem."

"Bye, cutie!" Tabitha waved her hand at him seductively.

After he left Felicia, he bobbed his way toward the VIP. He scanned through the crowd and noticed a group of South Siders in one of the VIP sections. As he walked over, he spotted Tyreek sitting next to some thick red-boned chick and he made his way through the crowd.

The South Side Boys was about 40 deep in VIP. Logik gave at least 20 people handshakes and hugs as he made his way towards the birthday boy. He spotted JuJu leaned back on the plush red couch with some big booty young chick on her knees between his legs topping him off.

He threw his hand up at JuJu, then turned around and found a seat in one of the lounge chairs. He grabbed one of the champagne glasses on the table, popped the top of the Rosè, and got it in with the rest of the homies.

About an hour and a half later, the DJ played Lil Jon and the Eastside Boys, "Throw Your Hood Up." Halfway through the song, the dance floor broke out in pandemonium. The drama that was going on did not involve the South Side Boys, so they continued smoking and drinking as they watched the action from the VIP section.

"Fuck!" Logik blurted out, as he passed the blunt of loud he was smoking to the dude next to him. "Yo, I gotta go find Felicia's ass!" He said out loud to no one in particular.

"Fuck that, we gone go wit'cha homey." Volunteered Gutta, referring to himself and the other two South Siders who was standing next to him and Logik at the time.

"Yeah, a'ight, whateva." Logik non-chalantly replied, then stormed out of VIP with three South Siders tailing him.

He squeezed through the thick crowd searching frantically for Felicia. He made it to the bar where they spoke earlier, but Felicia was nowhere in sight. They followed Logik outside then all four of them began searching the parking lot for Felicia. She was Bank's young and only sister, so Gutta and the other two dudes knew exactly how Felicia look as well.

It seemed as if shit was about to pop off in the parking lot as well because two small group of dudes was yelling and throwing up gang signs at each other. As they walked down each row of cars searching for Felicia, Logik saw a dude with a black bandana tied over his nose and mouth sliding a banana-looking clip into an AK-47. Since he was already in the parking lot, common sense told him that he needed to head to his own car and grab the Desert Eagle he had locked inside his glove compartment.

"I know ya'll saw ol'boy in back of that whip we just passed loading up a choppa?" Logik asked soon as they passed ol'boy. "Yo, I'm bout to shoot to the Lex real quick and grab my shit. I ain't leaving this mufucking parking lot til I make sure Felicia good."

"Yo, my truck right ova there. I'm 'bout to go snatch my shit up too." Gutta added, right before him, Jamal, and Shi-Hood stepped off.

As Logik sat sideways in the Lexus with the passenger door half way open, he remembered that he had Felicia's number saved in his cell phone. He pulled out his phone, scrolled down his contact list until he found her number, then hit Felicia up. He put the phone on speaker and sat it on the dashboard allowing it to ring as he tucked the Desert Eagle in his waistband.

"Hello!"

"This Logik, Felicia. Where you at girl?"

"Me and Tabitha just left the club, why?"

"Oh, nah. Just tryna make sure you straight. Soon as shit got crazy, I went and..."

BOC! BOC! BOC! BOC! BOC!

BOC! BOC! BOC!

Logik quickly ducked down in the car when the shooting started. Soon as the shooting stopped, he leaned up with the Eagle in his hand. His eyes roamed over the parking lot trying to locate his bomeboyz and also locate where the shots was being fired from. Majority of the people in the parking lot was either taking cover behind something, or trying to get far away from the shooting as possible, via car or foot.

The police must was already in the area because a few minutes after the shooting stopped, three police cruisers rushed into the parking lot. Gutta gestured to Logik with his hand from behind the steering wheel of his truck that he was about to leave then he pulled off in his Tahoe. Logik slid over into the driver's seat, put the key into the ignition, and did likewise.

Nights like this was the norm at many clubs in the Queen City.

Chapter 14

5 Months Later

THE FEBRUARY WIND rushed his face soon as he got out of his car. It had been five months since the "Block Party Massacre." Besides two girls from the South Side getting jumped at the car wash, a big fight between dudes from the North and South Side at a club, and the loss of Big E and Company. For the most part, the beef between the two sides had finally subside.

Logik was about to walk into the county jail to visit Black. For the past three months he had been visiting Black at least once a month and also helped to make sure his legal affairs was in order. Shortly after the "Block Party Massacre," he went to visit Black. Black had watched the news on his cell block concerning the massacre on the West side of the city.

Three days afterwards, Logik had came to visit him. When he asked Logik (speaking in codes) was anybody from their hood responsible for the massacre. Logik didn't answered. He just stared at Black with a smirk on his face, then winked his eye at him. At that moment, Black knew without a doubt that Logik was the man that the news said who was dressed in all black.

He uncomfortably waited in the visitation booth on the C.O. to bring out Black. He looked at several other visitors who was there visiting their loved ones. One girl was sitting in the visitor's booth holding a young child in her arm. Logik figured that she probably was there to visit the child's father.

Right then, he swore to himself that his child would never have to visit him inside no one's jailhouse. He snapped out of his thoughts when the C.O. entered the visitation room with Black. Black found the correct booth and sat down.

"What it is homey?" Logik cheerfully spoke, glad to see his comrade but hated that it had to be under those circumstances.

"Ain't shit, bro. 'Bout ready to knock off one of these faggot ass C.O.s out, that's it!" Black replied loudly, hoping the male C.O. heard him before he left the room.

Logik snickered, "I feel ya."

"But yo, how everything going wit Jazmine and the pregnancy? I hope you ain't stressing sis' ass out?"

"Eh'thang straight. She good, we good."

"That's wassup."

Oh, yeah. I forgot to mention, Jazmine was four months pregnant too. She had missed her menstruation period two months in a row and decided to buy a pregnancy test, because she never missed two months straight before. Two lines had showed up on the test stick indicating that she was pregnant. She wanted to be sure that the test hadn't made a mistake, so she went back to the drug store and bought another one. The outcome of the second test was the same.

"Yo, what ya'll lawyers saying about 'chall getting a bond though?" Asked Logik. Black, Mouse, and Twan's bond had been denied at their last arraignment. The prosecutor "highly" requested that their bonds all be denied because they were a "serious threat to society." And of course, the judge complied.

"He talking like we might be straight when we go back up the end of next month," he shrugged his shoulders. "I don't know, homey. Guess we'll see?"

Logik shook his head.

"Man, my muthafucking lawyer tryna tell me that the best option I got is to cop to 30 years."

Logik shook his head again. "Why he saying some shit like that for?" Logik asked, but deep inside he already knew the answer to his own question.

"He talking 'bout they got overwhelming evidence against me and that if I take the shit to trial and lose, I'll fuck round and get a LWOP," he replied. A LWOP was "Life Without Parole."

Logik could see tears building up in Black's eyes, but they went away soon as he started back talking.

"I don't know bro. Them pigs got two witnesses that picked all three of us out in a police line-up and everything."

Logik's eyebrow raised. "Okay then, who the witnesses is?" He inquired knowing the motto, "No face, no case."

"I already know what you're thinking dog, but that shit ain't gone eliminate our problems homey. The pigs got our prints all over them guns we tossed before they bagged us and I don't think I have to explain to you what the muthafuckin SLED laboratory said about them guns do I?"

Logik sighed deeply, feeling defeated. He wanted to tell Black that if they had fell back liked he had told all of them to do, that they wouldn't be in the shit they was in now. But he chose to keep his thoughts to himself because what was now understood should not be explained or reminded.

The visit with Black had been a painful one. It seemed that his comrade was stuck between a rock and a hard place, with no chance of escape anytime soon. With Banks dead and Black trapped in the belly of the beast, Logik felt empty in the streets.

He decided to call Jazmine on her phone to see how her day was going as he cruised down Atlantic Avenue. He had a lovely evening prepared for them and he also had a surprise for Jazmine as well. Logik was going to propose to her that night.

Their relationship had gotten much better and Logik hadn't slept with any other woman besides Jazmine in the past three months. He was tired of disrespecting her and was striving to be the man she needed because since day one, she damn sure been the kind of woman he needed. He dialed Jazmine's number and she picked up on the first ring.

"Hey, Babe!" She said as soon as she pressed talk on her phone.

"Wassup, Booski?" Booski had been a pet name he gave her shortly after they first met. "Where you at?"

"Oh, getting out the car 'bout to walk into Subway." She replied as she closed the door and chirped the alarm.

Logik snickered, "I see you still craving them subs and shit?"

"I know, right? I don't know why but..." She stopped in midsentence and turned her nose up as she walked. "Man, I know this gotta be my third time seeing that car today."

"What car, Jaz? What the car look like?" He asked nervously, immediately becoming worried.

"Ahh, it look like that car Bank's momma use to drive, but its dark blue though." She replied as the car passed her, and the driver trying his best to avoid eye contact with her.

Logik knew that she was referring to a Chevy Malibu. "You see who driving, Jaz?" He asked.

"Some guy, I don't know?"

"He look like Five-O or what?"

"I don't know boy, it's like three people in the car."

"Yo, what Subway you at? I'm on my way."

"I'm at the one in front of Westchester Mall," she replied. "But you ain't gotta worry 'bout coming though, cuz they just left out of the parking lot."

"It don't matter, I'm still coming!" He assured her.

She opened the door to Subway and walked in. "Don't worry 'bout it, Babe. I'm good. If I see the car again, I'll call you."

He started to protest, but changed his mind. For all he knew, the people in the car could've been undercover agents following her, hoping she lead them to him.

He sighed deeply. "A'ight then." He bypassed the exit he would've had to get off on had he been going to the Subway Jazmine was at. "Yo, I just had called to check up on ya'll and hear your voice."

She smiled because she knew that when he said "Ya'll," that he was referring to her and their child inside of her stomach. "Awh, you so sweet, Babe." A few people in the restaurant was looking at her because she was smiling from ear to ear. "Thanks for calling to check up on us, Boo. I love you, Jermaine." She cooed.

He smiled. "I love you too, Booski," he replied, not knowing that that would be the last time that either one of them would tell each other those beautiful words again.

Chapter 15

"I DON'T KNOW 'bout this country shit, Big Bro. Me and Budda had shit popping over there on Regal Street," said Marcus as he tried his best to reason with Logik. They was standing around the kitchen table in their new trap house. Logik had shut down their trap house on Regal Street and moved Marcus and Budda's operation out to a single-wide trailer in the country.

"It might take a week or two, but shit gone pop out here too. That spot on Regal Street done got extra hot since I hit ya'll with them 20 pounds of green. That dope money and weed money all coming to the same spot in the heart of the city ain't a good look," he explained. "Hell nah! Ya'll niggaz need to be right out here in this country where ya'll ain't got muthafuckin neighbors all up in ya'll bizness."

"I see what you saying, Big Dog, but I kinda feel where Marcus coming from though," Budda co-signed. "Ever since you started hitting us wit a halfa bird a piece, and them twenty pounds you gave us, shidd, money been pouring in like crazy."

"And money still gone pour in nigga! Have I steered ya'll niggaz wrong yet?" asked Logik.

"Nah!" They said in unison.

"A'ight then! Now, I told ya'll I got this weed connect now and I'mma be hitting ya'll wit as much grass as ya'll niggaz can cut." He took a long drag on the purple cush he was smoking then continued, "Ya'll just line ya'll clientele up and let'em know that ya'll done relocated and fuck all them small change muthafuckas. If they ain't buying a pound of green or a ounce of coke or better, then let somebody else get that chump change. Ya'll niggaz done graduated from all that petty shit."

They both nodded their heads in agreement.

"I'm about to pass the torch to ya'll in a few more months anyway. My muthfuckin seed on the way and I'm tryna put a ring on Jazmine's finger before she bring my seed into the world. Ya'll must think I'm playing bout opening up my own club and clothes store, huh?" He asked right after he had got finished dropping some jewels on them. That was also the other surprise he had in store for Jazmine later on that night. He was going to tell her that in three more months, he was getting out of the drug game permanently.

"Nah, Big Bro! I already know you ain't bullshitting about that," Marcus said truthfully.

"Word!" Budda co-signed. "Shid, I can't wait til you do that shit though, homey. I'm tryna feel what it's like to hold that torch you talking about my nigga!" Budda exclaimed sarcastically, but sincerely.

"That's what I'm talking bout!" Marcus added as he and Budda slapped each other's hand.

Logik chuckled as he reached into his pocket and grabbed his phone because it had started to ring. He saw that it was Jazmine, so he answered it, "What it is, Lil' Mama?"

"Nah, this aint'cha mama. This somebody you about to make rich, or you ain't gone never see this lil' fine ass bitch I got right here again!"

Logik's eyes stretched wide and his heart dropped to the bottom of his stomach.

"What's wrong, Big Bruh!?" Marcus asked, seeing the expression on Logik's face.

Logik ignored Marcus. "Yo, this some game or summin nigga!? Put Jazmine on the phone, clown!" He asked the male caller, not wanting to believe the obvious.

"Oh, you think this shit a game, huh!?"

...SMACK!!

Logik heard Jazmine howled and writhe in pain. His knees became weak and his legs buckled, causing him to drop down in the chair at the kitchen table.

"Yo, wassup bruh!?" Budda nervously asked.

Logik quickly put a finger to his lips, gesturing for Budda to be quiet.

"Now, you still think shit a game muthafucka!?" The caller asked.

"Nah homey, I believe you! Jjjust calm down dog and tell me what you want!?" He asked, trying his best to listen to the noise in the background on the other end of the phone.

Logik could hear the dude smiling on the other end of the phone.

"That's more like it," he sounded calmer. "I know you a business man and everything, so Ima just get skrait down to the business wit'cha...five hundred thousand. That's what it's gonna cost to get this pretty ass bitch of yours back. Yo, anybody ever told you your bitch look just like, Nia Long?" he asked with a sinister grin on his face. "I bet'cha she got some good pussy between them legs too?"

"Yo, chill out homey!" Logik barked. The tension seemed so thick it was buzzing in his ears.

"Nahh! You chill out mufucka, and get me what I asked for!"

Logik wiped the sweat from his brow with the back of his hand.

"Look, dog. I don't even got the type of paper you asking for. All I got is about..."

"Five hunnid thou muthfucka! This shit is non-negotiable!" He yelled with venom in his voice.

Marcus and Budda looked on in a state of confusion.

"A'ight, calm down dog...It's gone take me some time to come up with that type of bread you talking bout. Ima need at least..."

"It's almost three o'clock now. You got until midnight nigga. So you betta hurry up and start selling them bricks you got."

I better hurry up and start selling them bricks I got...This gotta be somebody that been watching me close? Logik thought to himself.

"A'ight, a'ight, chill nigga. When I get this money, what you want me to do with it?" Asked Logik. He could tell by the sounds in the background that they were travelling in some type of vehicle.

"I want you to hold it. I'll call you back at midnight and let you know what to do. Now, I ain't gone preach to you none of that shit. But you already know what the outcome gone be for your bitch if you get Five-O involved, right?"

"Fuck the police, I'mma street nigga!"

The dude chuckled. "Good for you." He hung up, then threw Jazmine's cell phone out of the car's window he was riding in.

Logik let his phone drop out of his hand onto the kitchen's table.

"Wassup, Big Bruh!?" Marcus asked with a concerned look on his face.

"They got Jazmine, yo." He replied in a defeated tone. Logik said "they" because he figured that it was more than one person involved in the kidnapping of his girl and his unborn child. He also remembered the three guys in the Malibu who Jazmine thought was following her.

"Who got, Jazmine, yo?" Inquired Budda.

"I don't know, dog? Some muthafucka just hit me from Jazmine's phone saying they want a halfa mill by midnight or else." The left side of his chest was pounding so hard, he was having complications breathing. He started massaging the side of his head with both hands.

"You already know if you ain't got that shit homey, we'll turn this city upside down and shake that muthafucka until a halfa mill fall out that bitch!" Marcus promised, meaning every word of it, ready to ride or die for the only nigga who saw the potential in him and Budda and had put both of them on.

Logik looked at Marcus, then dropped his head back don. He admired the loyalty in his words.

"Word, dog," Budda agreed with Marcus. He walked over and put his right hand on Logik's shoulder. "Look, homey. I know this shit got you messed up right now, but we ain't got no time to sit round here feeling sad 'bout this shit. We need to get up out of here and go get that bread up dog. Unless you got that type of paper on deck already?" Budda spoke the truth.

That call had seemed to knock all the energy out of Logik, but nevertheless, he knew that Budda had spoken truthfully. Logik only had about one hundred and seventy thousand dollars and four bricks to his name. He knew that if he drop the price on the bricks, would be able to sell all four of them in less than a hour.

He grabbed his phone and stood up from the table.

"Look, yo. Ya'll go head and pack all this shit up while I step outside and make a few calls. After ya'll finish that, ya'll go head and hit ya'll peoples up and sell them all the work ya'll got for the low. I need to get up as much paper as possible because I don't got five hundred thousand." Logik told them both, referring to all the cocaine and pounds of weed that was stacked neatly on top of the kitchen table.

"That's wassup, Big Bruh." Budda replied, then he and Marcus started doing as they was told.

Logik walked outside and hpped into his Lexus that was parked on the grass in the front yard.

The first person he called was a dude name T-Bird who he did business with.

"Yo!" T-Bird said when he answered his phone.

"Peace, homey."

"Oh, whut up my nigga?"

"Maintaining," replied logic before he got down to business. "Yo, check. I got a block of concrete for your house that I'll let you get for twenty-three homey. This a one time deal." Logik spoke in codes letting T-Bird know that he had a brick for twenty-three thousand dollars. Usually, Logik sold a brick for thirty-thousand.

"Hmm," T-Bird starting calculating how much money he had. "Shidd, if it's like that. Let me get two of them joints then. That's all I can stand right now."

"Bet! Meet me in the parking lot of the old Chinese restaurant that burnt down on Nelson Ave in like 45 minutes. And stay there til I get there. I'm kinda on the move right now." Logik instructed.

"I'll be there."

"Peace."

Two down. Two to go.

Logik scrolled down his contact list until he found Junior's number, then he hit him up.

"Hello."

"Peace, homey."

"Peace, peace. Wassup wit it, cuz?" Junior asked, speaking in his "Crip" lango. Logik never could understand how Junior could call everybody his cousin. Junior was telling him a story one time how he had beat a nigga's ass he caught creeping out of his kid's mother's house before. And Junior even referring to that dude as his cousin too.

"I'm cooling. Check it out though. I got this once-in-a-lifetime deal for you. I'm tryna get rid of all this old concrete in my yard and I'll let you get a block for the Michael Jordan." He told Junior, offering him the same price as he did T-Bird.

"Dayum! That's love right there, cuz. What's the catch?"

"Ain't no catch nigga. I'm just tryna stack some chips up real quick. Now, you tryna fuck wit it or not?"

"Yeah, I'mma fuck wit'cha, cuz." Junior assured.

"A'ight. Meet me at Eastwood Park on the gym side in 45 minutes. And stay put until I get there."

"That's wassup, cuz."

"And I ain't yo cousin, fool!" Logik said, then hung up before Junior could reply.

Three down. One to go.

He then called a chick he knew and ended up selling her the last brick he had. Soon as he got off the phone with her. Marcus and Budda came out of the front door. Budda made his way towards the Lexus with a blue gym bad in hand, while Marcus was locking the front door with the house key.

A few minutes later, they was on the interstate.

"Here you go, Big Homey." Marcus said, passing Logik a brown paper bag with money in it, as Logik drove.

"What's this?" He quizzically asked.

"That's thirty-three bands right there. Twenty of that is money we owed you. The other thirteen is me and Budda's money." Marcus explained. "Plus the work we got in the bookbag. Soon as you finish handling your bizness, we can shoot to a few of our people's spots and get rid of the rest of this shit."

"That's peace, dog. Yo," Logik handed Marcus the bag of money back. "Put that shit in the glove compartment."

Budda was in the backseat rolling up a needed blunt for all of them.

"Ya'll niggaz kept shit one thousand wit me since day one...Soon as this shit over with and I get back on my feet, ya'll already know I'mma bless ya'll niggaz?" Logik glanced at Marcus, then looked at Budda in his reaview mirror.

"Fuck all that shit, Logik. Let's just worry 'bout getting your shorty and your seed back right now. We did whateva we did from the heart and ain't looking for shit in return for it my nigga."

Even though he felt horrible on the inside, Logik had to blush at Budda's words. His young gunner's loyalty to him was overwhelming.

Chapter 16

10:12 pm

"I STILL THINK some of them niggaz on the North Side got summin to do wit this shit." figured Budda. He had been trying to convince Logik for the past hour that he believed someone from the North Side was involved with the kidnapping of Jazmine.

They had already sold all of the product they had to their clients. The money they made off of the product, including all the money Logik had, totaled up to three-hundred and fourteen thousand dollars. Logik had been one-hundred and eighty-six thousand dollars short of the ransom money he needed to get Jazmine back, so he had hit Frank up for the rest. Frank was very reluctant at first about loaning Logik (or anyone for that matter) that amount of money. But when Logik explained the situation concerning what happened to Jazmine to him. Frank had sympathized with Logik and agreed to loan him the money, only if Logik agreed to pay him back with interest.

Logik had assured him that the kidnappers would let Jazmine go free once they got the money. But Frank knew the game and knew that Logik's chance of seeing his girl alive again was slim to none. Nevertheless, he wanted his money back, plus interest, or Logik's ass was going to be the next to get kidnapped.

Logik had wanted to contact Jazmine's mother and inform her about Jazmine, but he changed his mind. He couldn't bring himself to call her mother and tell her that something had happened to Jazmine because of his lifestyle.

That was definitely out of the question.

Now he was on his way to meet Frank and pick up the hundred and eighty-six thousand.

"I don't think so, lil' bro. That's not their style. If they wanted to get at me or anyone else, they woulda just pulled up and handle that shit on the site...Nah. Whoever involed wit this shit is somebody who know me very well."

"Whoever it is, when we find out. They might as well get ready to start pushing up flowers!" Marcus exclaimed.

"Soon as I get Jazmine back, hopefully she will be able to describe something about them dudes or something she saw that will help me out to identify them." Said Logik, still trying to keep hope alive as far as Jazmine's life was concern. The only suspects Logik had in mind at that moment was the unknown niggaz in the dark-blue Malibu.

He went quiet at the light. When it turned green he took off through a wide junction and hugged the right lane.

Twenty minutes later, they was parked at the self-serve car wash on Simpson Boulevard.

Logik got out of the Lexus, walked over and got inside Frank's black on black Audi A6.

"Wassup, Playboy?" Spoke Frank, reaching his hand out for Logik to shake.

"Wassup, Man?" Logik shook hands with Frank. Frank noticed how drained Logik had look. Not wanting to hold him up any longer. He reached between his legs, grabbed a small leather bag and tossed it on Logik's lap.

"I threw a extra four stacks in there to make it a even one-ninety. I figured once you get your lady back, that you might wanted to fall back and spend a little time with her before you get back on your grind?"

"That's good looking out right there, Frank. I won't forget this shit."

You bet not forget nigga, or I'mma murder you and your bitch for costing me almost two-hunnid bands. Frank thought to himself as he stared in Logik's eyes.

"No doubt, Playboy." Frank replied, instead of speaking what he was thinking.

They shook hands once again, then Logik lopped out of the Audi and headed back to his own car, where Marcus and Budda waited patiently.

11:15 pm

MARCUS AND BUDDA was sitting at the kitchen table in their new trapspot smoking a Bob Marley of some "fiyah" ass weed. They had been watching Logik pacing back and fourth in the living room mumbling to himself ever since they got back from meeting Frank.

Budda had been wanted to say something to Logik concerning what they're plan would be after he receive the call at midnight, but he decided to fall back because he figured that Logik would put them up on game later.

Fifteen more minutes would go by before Logik stopped pacing, and walked into the kitchen and sat down at the table in front of his soldier. The closer to midnight it got, the more nervous Logik became. He was staring out past Marcus and Budda and blinking, like he was about to cry. He then shook his head and tightened his lips to control his emotions.

Budda and Marcus hated seeing their Big Homey that way. They only could imagine what he was feeling on the inside.

Logik slowly rubbed both hands down his face before he spoke.

"I don't know what I'll do if summin happen to Jazmine and my seed man?" Logik said to himself.

"Don't even talk like that, Big Bruh." Budda said.

"Yeah, everything gone work out." Marcus added, not really believing his own words. He was just preparing himself for whatever the outcome may be.

Logik didn't respond. He just sat their quiet, in deep thought, while twirling one of his dreds around his finger.

Budda and Marcus both looked at each other and shook their heads, not knowing what else to say about it.

12:01 am

LOGIK WAS WATCHING the clock on his cell phone like a owl. He feared the worse when the kidnappers didn't call at exactly 12 o'clock like he said he would. He started to get up from the table and start pacing again when his phone suddenly rung.

The number was marked private.

"Yo!"

"You got my money?" He asked.

"Yeah, I got it."

"Good for you. Now, this is what I want you…"

"Yo, hold the fuck up nigga! You ain't got shit else to tell me unless I know for sure my girl still alive and ain't hurt!"

Silence.

"Hmm, okay. Guess you want some proof of life, huh?"

"Yeah, that's right."

"…Fair enough,"

Logik could hear the kidnapper in the background instructing Jazmine to tell him that she was okay, and for her not to say anything else.

"Hhello," Logik could hear the pain in Jazmine's voice when she spoke into the phone.

Logik's eyes stretched wide. "Jaz!" He said excitedly. "Did they hurt you? Are you okay?"

She sniffed then said. "Yeah, I'm okay…Baby its, Pea…"

WHOPP!!

"Hard-headed ass bitch!"

SMACK!! WHOPP!!

"Jazmine!!" Logik yelled into the phone, as he jumped up from the table. "Yo, Jaz!! Eh, muthfucka!! Leave my girl alone you bitch ass nigga!! I got'cho fucking money!!" Logik's bronze skin complexion started to turn a different color.

Marcus and Budda looked on with a angry look on their face.

"Hello!…Helloo!"

"Yeah, I'm here dude. Stop all that fucking yelling in my ear." He said calmly, like he hadn't just got finish busting Jazmine's face up.

"What the fuck you did to my girl!"

"Eh, eh, ehh!!"

CLICK CLACK!

Logik heard him jacked a round into the chamber of his gun.

"You must want me to kill this bitch!?" He asked. "Now, I'm done playing games wit'cha ass motherfucker! Either you gone listen to where I want you to drop my money off at, or I'mma just go ahead and kill the bitch and find another baller's bitch to kidnap!" He called Logik's bluff.

Logik knew he wasn't in a position to give orders, so he decided to calm down before he got Jazmine killed.

"A'ight, go head and say whut'chu gone say."

"My man," Dude said, sounding like Denzel Washington off of Training Day. "Here is what I want you to do…"

LOGIK RODE BY himself down the highway, with Marcus and Budda following behind him in Budda's Infiniti. He had all the windows in the Lexus wound all the way down (despite the fact that it was 48 degrees outside). The cold wind that blew through the windows didn't faze him, because he was burning up on this inside and his blood pressure was through the roof.

The kidnapper told Logik that he wanted him to drive to Ashely Park, drop the bag of money inside a trash can that would have red tape wrapped around it, and then leave. He told Logik that he would call him 15 minutes after the drop-off and let him know how to find Jazmine.

He had no way to know for certain if he would find Jazmine alive or not, other than dropping the money off and waiting on the kidnapper to call him with the directions.

But that is the kidnapper even call at all.

Logik put his hand out the window, signaling to Budda that he was about to pull over. He braked and eased right onto the shoulder of the road. He feathered the pedal and coasted to a stop in a big cloud of dust. He got out and walked to the passenger's side of the Infiniti.

Marcus wound the window down.

"Here, take this." Said Logik, as he gave Marcus his binocular. "I know ya'll should be familiar wit Ashley Park, right?"

They both nodded, "Yeah."

"A'ight, check it out. I want ya'll to go to that Exxon gas station that's a little ways down from the park, and park right there by the phone booth. Ya'll should be able to see inside the park good as a muthafucker with them binoculars right there." He nodded to the binocular in Marcus' hand. "I don't know if ya'll gone be able to see me the whole time or not because I don't even know which trash can in the park they want me to drop the bag in...But if I had to guess, I bet'chu that that trashcan somewhere towards the back of the park, far away from the street as possible." Logik shook his head, puzzled. "But ya'll know I got the heat wit me and I'mma have my phone on inside my hoodie, so if ya'll niggaz hear some funny shit. Then ya'll already know what to do."

"Yo, I don't know why you just can't let one of us go wit'chu to drop that bread off, Big Bruh" Said Marcus.

Budda nodded. "Word."

"Look, I ain't tryna do nuttin' else to tick these muthfuckers off. I'm pretty sure they got somebody out there somewhere watching my every move. All them fools care about is that paper, and I seriously doubt it that they'll waste their time bodying me."

"I feel that, but you still gotta keep in mind that you don't know who these dudes is. For all you know these muthafuckas could be somebody that want your money and your life. You never know, Big Bruh." Budda wisely spoke.

Logik had already thought of that, but his mind was made up.

"Yeah, I understand all of that, but I just want ya'll niggaz to do what I asked ya'll to do. A'ight?"

They both reluctantly nodded their heads.

"A'ight," Logik said, then walked back to his car.

Five minutes later, they was turning on the street that the park was located on. Budda put his left signal on and blew past Logik's Lexus, heading for the Exxon. Logik put his left signal on as he approached the park, then turned into the entrance. He parked the car, grabbed the gym bag, and got out.

He spotted two trash cans that was in front of him. Neither one of them had red tape wrapped around it, so he past them by and proceeded towards the back of the park. He saw another trashcan that was by the jungle-gym, but it didn't had red tape around it, so he kept moving.

Before long, he saw the trash can that had the tape around it. So he walked over and dropped the bag inside of it.

"There goes everything I got." Logik thought to himself as he walked back to his car.

He hopped into his car, then took a right turn out of the park and headed back down the street that he initially came from. He pulled out his cell phone and dialed Budda's number.

"Yeah, we saw you homey. We pulling up out this bitch now. We'll be behind you in a second." Budda said soon as he answered the phone.

"A'ight," Logik replied, then hung up.

After Logik got a few blocks away from the park, he decided to pull into KFC's parking lot and park. A minute later, Budda pulled in and parked beside the Lexus. Logik got out and hopped into the backseat of Budda's Infiniti.

No one spoke when he got in.

Logik sat there impatiently quiet and nervous as hell. He had his cell phone in his left hand, and was twirling one of his dreds around a finger on his right hand. Something he also did when he was in deep thought.

Then his phone rung.

The caller ID showed that the number was marked Private.

"Yo, hello!"

"My man. I see that you a man of your word," The dude said referring to the money that one of his partners had just got out of the trash can in the park after Logik left. The dude's partner had been laying inside one of the sliding tubes in the jungle gym watching Logik's every move. "I guess you wanna know where yo bitch at now, right?" He asked devilishly.

"Yeah, nigga! I already did my part, now where she at!" Logik was vexed.

"Calm down baby boy, calm down. I got'chu," He assured. "You know where the shelter at on Livingston Street?"

"Yeah, I know where that at."

"Well, it's an abandoned building that sits diagonal about 50 yards in front of the shelter. If you walk to the back of the building, you'll find that I left one of the doors halfway opened for you. Once you go inside and look round for a bit, you'll find your pretty little girlfriend. Now hate to run, baby boy. But as you already know. I got a lotta muthafucking paper to count! It was nice doing business with you my man." He snickered, then hung up. He gestured with his head to the other dudes who was standing by him for them to leave. They walked out the building. Leaving the door halfway open.

Chapter 17

THE SHARP, PUNGENT odor of urine, mold, and some more shit filled the inside of the building and turned Logik's stomach soon as he walked through the door. The only light in the building was that of the light poles on the street, which shined through the cracks in the boarded up building.

The building use to be a bus station back in the 70's before it closed.

The trio had their guns in hand as they carefully searched each area of the building, ready to blast anybody that wasn't Jazmine. A jumbo-sized sewer rat startled Logik and caused him to aim his weapon when it ran past him. They continued their search, all the while listening for sounds of anything other than that of creeping rodents.

"Eh, Jaz-mine!..Jaz-mine!" Hollered Logik as he studied his surroundings and waited for a response.

He heard none. So they continued searching the place.

They opened up each door that they passed, entering the rooms and aiming their weapons around like SLED in a drug bust. The door to the next room they walked up on was already opened so they walked in.

The gun in Logik's hand dropped to the floor, and his eyes got big as saucers when he saw Jazmine's body sprawled out on the floor in a pool of blood.

"Oh no!" He yelled. "Jazmine!" You could hear the pain in his voice when he cried her name out. Marcus kneeled down and picked up his gun as Logik ran towards Jazmine. Budda stayed posted by the doorway with his gun in hand.

The worse has finally happened.

Logik dropped down to his knees in the pool of blood. Marjority of the blood had been pouring from Jazmine's neck, and her head was tilted to the side awkwardly. He started examining her body closely. He noticed that her face was badly bruised and her neck had been roughly sliced from ear to ear. The bloodstains on her face was already drying and blackening. Her pink Gucci purse was a few feet away from her body on the floor.

Logik sobbed loudly as he laid his head on her chest and wrapped his arm around her belly. He knew that she was dead because she wasn't breathing and he felt no movement on the left side of her chest.

Marcus walked over and picked up Jazmine's purse that was on the floor. He saw that her credit and identification cards was still on the inside. He wiped his prints off of everything he touched and threw the purse back on the floor.

"Better to let the police find it. That way, they'll know who she is when they find the body." Thought Marcus.

"Come on baby, get up," Logik kissed her on the cheek. "We gotta get outta here before the cops come, Ma. We gotta get'chu outta these bloody clothes baby." Logik was very delusional. "Don't worry bout it though. I'mma take you shopping and buy you one of them expensive ass designer dresses. Mmm-hmm. I'mma get'chu some Chanel shades, and them new Chanel boots you said you had liked, Ma." He started chuckling. "Them bitches really gone hate on you then baby." Logik had a smile on his face at the time like he was having a full blown conversation with Jazmine.

Budda made eye contact with Marcus, gesturing to him with his eyes that it was time to snap Logik out of his psychotic state of mind so they could leave.

"We gotta get outta here, Logik. We can tell the cops from a pay phone or summin, but we need to bounce man." Budda said loud enough for him to hear.

Marcus kneeled down and placed a hand on Logik's back. "She gone, Big Bro." Marcus added, hoping his words brought Logik back to reality.

"I can't leave her, man. I can't leave her like this, yo." Replied Logik, sounding like he was about the breakdown in tears again.

Marcus shook his head. "You ain't gotta leave her, Big Bro...cause she already gone."

The sounds of sirens could be heard in the distance.

"I hear police sirens, yo! We need to get the fuck outta here ya'll!" Budda shouted.

Marcus shook Logik. "We gotta bounce, dog. The muthafucking police might be coming here, Logik! Let's go man, lets go!" Marcus yelled with authority in his voice.

Logik snapped back into reality.

The sirens was getting closer.

"Lets go!" Budda shouted again.

Marcus then started lifting Logik off of Jazmine.

"Yo, her ID and shit over there in her purse homey," Marcus pointed to Jazmine's purse on the floor. "The cops will know who she is when they find that shit, bruh. But we need to raise up outta here, man." Logik reluctantly allowed Marcus to help him up. The left side of his face was covered in Jazmine's blood.

The trio then made their way out the building and ran down the street.

Logik steopped in mid-stride when he saw that the police cruiser passed by the building, obviously heading to another location. Logik wanted to go back to lay next to Jazmine's body.

Marcus and Budda stopped running when he did. The look on Logik's face told them that he wanted to go back to the building.

"Logik! Let's go man. We'll go to a pay phone and send the ambulance to Jazmine, man. Ain't nutting else we can do for her my nigga."

Logik wanted to protest, but he changed his mind and decided to follow Budda's advice.

They pulled into 7 Eleven's parking lot and parked in front of the phone booth. Budda got out and made the anonymous call to 911, letting the operator know where they could find a dead body at.

After that, Budda told Logik to follow behind him. Minutes later, they pulled into Sleep Inn's parking lot. Budda went to the service window and rented a double bedroom for one night.

They pulled around the back and parked in front of room 201. They all got out and went inside. Logik plopped down on the edge of the bed, slumped his shoulders and stared at the carpet on the floor.

Marcus pulled a cigar out of the half-filled 50 pack Swisser Sweet box and rolled up. They ended up smoking several blunts of purple haze and demolishing the fifth of Remy that Buddda had in his car.

A LITTLE AFTER 3 o'clock that morning. Jazmine's mother, Ms. Wanda, received a disturbing call from a Detective Karen McKullard informing her about her daughter's death. She agreed to meet Detetive McKullard down at the morgue so she could identify the body.

A hour later (after positively identifying Jazmine's corpse), a hysterical Ms. Wanda sat inside Detective McKullard's car and tried her best to answer each question the Detective and her partner was asking her. Ms. Wanda told them about her daughter and Logik's relationship and also about his criminal activities. She told them that she don't believe that Logik killed her daughter, but that she do believe that he knew who did though.

Once Detective McKullard and her partner Peter Finch finished interviewing Ms. Wanda. She dialed the number that Ms. Wanda gave them, which belonged to Logik. Even though it was about 4:15 am, It was still better to question a suspect or a witness earliest as possible because details would be fresher in one's mind after a crime happened.

Detective McKullard was shocked when Logik actually answered the phone. She first told him about Jazmine, then she told him that she would like for him to meet her at the police station for questioning because they needed to find out who murdered his girlfriend in such a cruel way. Logik told her that after hearing such news about his girlfriend that he wasn't in a "question asking mood." Detective

McKullard said she understood and gave Logik her cell and office number. He agreed to meet her at the precinct a 1 pm.

Detective McKullard hit the end button on her cell phone. She turned and faced her partner who was sitting in the passenger seat. "This guy is definitely hiding something." Detective Finch seemed unsurprised by her statement. In his eyes, all Blacks were guilty.

MARCUS WAS THE first to wake up. After he got finished using the bathroom, he went and woke Budda only, because he thought it was best to let Logik rest. Instead, he grabbed a pen off the dresser and decided to leave Logik a short note.

Yo, Big Bro. Me and Budda got some moves we need to make. We know a few pussy niggaz we gone shake down for some paper since shit fucked up right now. So go head and fall back and get'cha mind right homey. We gonna keep the trap house bumping. Don't even stress that! Anyway, we both got our phones on, so hit us up if her decide to get into something.

-Love Homey!

Marcus then took some of the hotel's generic brand toothpaste, put some on the back of his letter, and pasted it to the door. It would be impossible for Logik to miss that when he woke up.

The loud humming sound from a vacuum cleaner woke Logik. When he fully became conscious, he realized that housekeeping was in the room next door cleaning up. He had a massive headache and the veins on the side of his head was throbbing painfully.

He noticed that Marcus and Budda had already left. When he looked at the door, he saw the letter Marcus had left there, so he got up and went to get it. After he finished reading it, he went into the bathroom to take a piss. As he was relieving himself. The pain from the loss of Jazmine was starting to creep up on him again.

He forgot that he had turned his phone off, so he grabbed it off the nightstand and turned it back on. He had 9 missed calls. 2 from Frank, 3 was from a few of his clients calling for some work, and 4 from his aunt Vanessa. He decided he would holla at Frank about the money situation later, so he hit his Aunt Vanessa up.

"Hello,"

"Sup, Auntee. You hit me up?"

"Damn right I hit you up! Where the hell you at boy?"

He noticed the urgency and nervousness in her tone.

"I'm around, wassup?" He quizzically asked.

"Well, yo ass might don't need to be around," She said. "The damn po-lice had my muthafucking house surrounded, and they came up in this bitch with a search warrant looking for drugs and your ass. I thank God ain't nuttin been up in this muthafucker though. Where you at boy?"

"I'll rather not say," He started thinking. "Did them muthafuckas say exactly what they been looking for me for?"

"They ain't say, Jermaine. All they said was that they had a warrant for your arrest."

Logik started thinking.

What was crazy is that he was actually about to go down to the precinct in a couple of hours to speak with Detective McKullard.

And that bitch talking 'bout she wanna ask me some questions bout Jazmine's murder? That lying ass bitch! She ain't gotta worry bout seeing my face no time soon though. I gotta find out who these pussy as niggaz is that killed my babe first. Logik thought to himself.

"Look, Auntie. I gotta hang up now. I'll contact you if I need summin. Don't let nobody know you heard from me, okay?" He decided he will tell her about Jazmine later.

She sighed. "Okay, baby. You be careful, you hear?"

"You know that." He assured her before he hung up.

Logik sat on the side of the bed with a puzzled look on his face. With the police now looking for him, finding the people who was involved in Jazmine's murder had just became more complicated. Not to mention that he owed Frank $190,000 plus interest. But finding out who killed Jazmine and his unborn child was more important than the money he owed Frank at the time.

A decision that would come with a deadly price.

Logik knew that he needed something other than his Lexus to get around in, but all he had was $72 to his name. He grabbed the hotel's phone that was on the nightstand beside the bed and called his cousin Melinda.

She picked up on the fourth ring.

"Hello,"

"Sup, kuzzo?"

"Who this, Jermaine?" She asked, recognizing his voice but not the phone number that showed up on her caller ID.

"Who it sound like girl? You at the house?"

She yawned. "Yeah, wassup?" She hoped that Logik wasn't calling because he wanted to cook up for him. Not that she didn't need the money, but she was clubbing all night and she was tired as hell.

"Yo, I need you to come pick me up from The Sleep Inn on Main Street."

"Dayum," She sounded aggravated. "What, you need me to come now?"

"Yeah," He paused. "I'm in room 201 in the back. I'll be looking out for you."

She yawned again. "I got'chu."

Forty-five minutes later, he saw Melinda's Nissan Altima creeping at a low-speed past the vending machines. He grabbed the room's card-key off of the table and walked out. Locking the door behind him. Melinda slowed to a stop when she saw Logik walking towards her car. She hit the unlock button on her door and he hopped in.

"What's good?"

"Ain't nuttin," she replied. Melinda had a housecoat on with a scarf on her head. Even though her hair was a mess under the scarf, her beauty was undeniable. "You okay?" She asked after she saw his serious looking face.

He ignored her question. "Look, I need to borrow your car for a day or two."

Melinda was thinking about lying and telling Logik that she had a doctor's appointment, but Logik had never asked for her car before. So she knew that whatever his reason was for wanting to borrow her car had to be important.

"When you need it?" She inquired as she made a left turn out of the hotel's parking lot and merge into traffic.

"A-SAP. But I need to get them guns I got stashed in your back yard first." He had a small arsenal of guns buried in Melinda's backyard. Most of which he bought from Ms. Pat.

Logik had done so many favors for her in the past that she couldn't complain. She just hoped that he return her car back to her in one piece.

She changed the subject.

"How many months is Jazmine now?" Asked Melinda unaware that she was inquiring about a dead woman.

Logik then gave her the scoop on Jazmine's death as they rode to her house, but he left out the part about her being kidnapped.

Melinda would pick his Lexus up from the hotel that next day.

Chapter 18

"UNBELIEVABLE! UN-FUCKING BELIEVABLE!" Fumed Detective Karen McKullard as she slammed the phone down. She was investigating the murder of Jazmine Sutton. Thus far, there was no leads in the case. But judging by everything she saw at the crime scene, there was a motive...

Money.

Her years of experience in law enforcement and expertise in investigating homicides lead her to believe that her victim had been kidnapped for a ransom, which was or was not paid by her drug dealing boyfriend.

Detetive Karen McKullard had just angrily hung the phone up on Lead Investigator Ted Conwell who worked in the Narcotics Division. She had learned from one of her confidential informants that her murder victim's boyfriend was a local drug dealer. So being that she already suspected that her victim had been held for a ransom, she figured that the person who was to pay that ransom was the victim's boyfriend, and also that he may have the answers that could lead to the suspect or suspects in the case. But when Ted told her that he and his team had just raided Logik's aunt's house two hours prior seeking to apprehend him on drug charges, Detective Karen McKullard had a fit.

Hopefully he'll meet me here as promised or they apprehend him before he find out about the raid and avoid being captured. Detective Karen McKullard thought to herself.

Her partner Detective Peter Finch walked back into the office with their cups of coffee.

"Here you go miss lady," He said as he sat a hot cup of coffee on the desk in front of her. "That'll be $1.69 young lady," He joked. The smile on his face disappeared when he saw the serious look on his partner's face. "Is everything alright, Karen?" Peter asked, taking a seat in front of her.

She went on to explain the phone call she had with Investigator Ted Conwell.

AFTER LOGIK LEFT the Verizon store, where he had purchased a new cell phone. HE called his cousin V-God in Brooklyn, New York.

"Wassup, kuzzo?"

"Who this?"

"This your cousin, Logik nigga. It ain't been that long fool." Logik replied, not understanding how his cousin couldn't recognize his voice.

"Oh, what's poppin sun!?"

"I'm cooling. Check it out though. You remember you asking me bout some hardware in the past and I told you that mechanics round my way don't get rid of shit like that?"

"Right, right." V-God remembered.

"Well, I know a mechanic who 'bout to close his shop down and he tryna sell majority of his tools." Logik was referring to the small arsenal of guns he now had in the truck of Melinda's car. He had kept a few guns in the cut for himself, but the rest had to go. He needed the money.

V-God smiled. "Trillz. What kind of tools he tryna sell fam?" V-God and some of his homies had beef with the Crips from Flatbush Avenue, so the extra guns would come in handy.

"The same type of shit you been asking about in the past."

"A'ight, what's the ticket on them joints then?" V-God wanted to know the price.

"A halfa chicken's worth. Trust. It's worth it," Logik told him that he wanted a half of brick of cocaine for the guns. "Plus deliver."

V-God was thinking.

"That's peace. How soon ya man talking bout, sun?"

"It's almost one o'clock now, so I'm guessing around eleven or twelve tonight."

"Trillz. Let him know I'm still in the same spot and to hit me up when he get on the block," V-God lived in Bed-Stuy, the same hood The Notorious Big was from.

"No doubt."

"Peace god," V-God fair-welled Logik in his Godbody lango. V-God was a member of The Nation, Gods, and Earth.

As Logik rode down I-95 North, on his way to the Big Apple. Thoughts of Jazmine, his unborn child, his mother, Banks, Champagne, The Block Party Massacre, and the fact that he was a "Wanted Man" was starting to make him stress. A cold chill ran through his body bringing him back from the place his mind was trying to take him.

10 hours later, Logik was coasting through the Holland Tunnel, cutting across Canal Street, and eventually crossing the Manhattan Bridge into Brooklyn, where V-God rested his head. Logik wasn't familiar with New York, but he knew the place he was going to like the back of his hand.

He turned left on Tompkins Avenue in Bed-Stuy and hit V-God's cell.

"Peace God!"

"Peace. Yo, I just turned on Tompkins." Logik told him as he drove pass a group of gangbangers who was staring daggers at the unfamiliar car with the out of state tags on it.

"Damn sun, you made it out the Tunnel already?" Asked V-God but didn't wait for an answer. "But yo, I'm out here though, B. Just keep coming down. Me and the gods standing out here in front of the bodega," He told Logik in his deep New York accent, his words coming in puffs of smoke from the winter air.

A few minutes later, he spotted V-God standing with a crowd of dudes in front of the bodega dressed in brown army fatigues and a pair of Wheat Timbs on his feet. He pulled up in front of the store and V-God hopped in.

"Long time no see sun. What's poppin beloved?" V-God asked as he gave his cousin Logik a handshake and brotherly hug.

"I'm maintaining, how you?" Asked Logik as they both looked at each other with smiles of their face. Happy to see one another.

"I'm living B. But true story, sun. We don't need to be politicking right here." He told logic, wanting to hurry up and leave from out front of the bodega. Logik eased into traffic behind a taxi cab.

Charlotte was big, but Brooklyn was HUGE. The high-rise buildings in the Big Apple had always mesmerized him.

V-God took a Newport from out of his pack and lit it. "How shit going for in the dirty south, B? This ain't 'cho style coming all the way up here for a halfa bird sun. Last time we spoke you been doing A'ight, B. What's really goody though?" V-God quizically asked, sensing that his cousin had financial problems. Logik briefly explained to him about Jazmine and the money he owed Frank.

"Yo, you know sun gone be thirty-eight hot bout them two hunnid racks you owe him? Niggaz'll merk ya whole family for that type of bread out here B." He said. "You need to let me go back down south wit'chu to help you put that work in, sun?" V-God sincerely offered, ready to ride or die with his blood.

"Trust me. I got plenty enough help back home. I just need to get my bread back up real quick while I find out who kilt Jazmine and my seed."

V-God nodded. "Yeah, I feel you my nigga. But don't sleep on sun who you owe them two hunnid racks to either. That nigga ain't gone wanna hear no stories on why you ain't got his bread." He forewarned Logik.

"Fuck that nigga dog! Either he wait til I pay him that shit back or we can hold court in the street! I really don't give a fuck!" Logik had a lot of shit on his mind and V-God was making his blood pressure go up bout Frank's money. "You act like my hammer don't pop or summin!?" Logik scolded him.

"Yo sun, you bugging! I already know how you give it up on the blacktop. You my blood, B. All I was doing was speaking out of love my nigga," V-God didn't like how Logik came out the mouth at him, but he knew that his cousin was under a lot of stress, due to all the drama he had going on. So he gave Logik a pass.

V-God decided to change the subject.

"But anyway, I got that halfa bird on me right now," He had the half of brick in Saran Wrap which was taped around his mid-section.

V-God looked up at the street signs and saw that they was approaching Marcus Garvey and Lewis. "Yo, make a right turn at this light." He instructed.

Logik put the right signal on and turned right. "My bad for spazing out on you bruh. My mind just fucked up right now." He told V-God.

He looked at Logik. "I can did that," V-God reached over and bumped a fist with Logik. "I really hate that you going through all this bullshit." V-God then reahed into his pocket and pulled out a wad of bills. He quickly counted out five-thousand dollars and handed it to Logik.

Logik looked at the money in his hand confusedly. "What's this for?"

"Yo, sun. That's the least I can do since you want let me go back wit'chu to body some of them country ass niggaz,"

Logik smiled. "Good looking out kuzza," They bumped fist.

"You ready."

"But yo, how much longer we gotta ride dirty around the city?" Inquired Logik, as he looked in his rearview mirror.

"We almost there B. I'm taking you to one of my duck off spots so I can stash these hammers, and then give you time to stash that snow somewhere in your ship before you get back on that highway."

"Yeah, A'ight." Replied Logik, while looking straight ahead, trying to make himself look inconspicuous because a blue and white NYPD cruiser was passing them in the left lane.

V-God looked over at Logik and chuckled because he knew that the infamous NYPD had his cousin paranoid.

Chapter 19

LOGIK HAD TOOK V-God's advice and stayed at his stash house a while, where he got six hours of some needed rest before he jumped back on the road. It was 8:23 pm when Logik pulled into Melinda's yard and parked.

He stepped out the car and stretched the kinks out of his body from sitting in one position for so many hours. Melinda looked through her window blinds and saw her car pulled into the drive-way. "Thank God," She said out loud, glad that Logik and her car made it back safely.

"'Bout time nigga! I started to file a missing person report on yo ass!" Melinda said jokingly, as she stood in the doorway smiling.

Logik ignored her sarcasm and handed her the keys to her car as he walked past her. "You got anything planned tonight?"

"Not really. I need to run to the grocery store and pick up a few packages, but other than that, I'm good." She replied then walked over and sat back down on the couch, so she could finish catching the rest of The Real Housewives of Atlanta that was on TV.

"Good," He dropped the half of bird that was wrapped in Saran Wrap next to her on the couch. "I'mma need you to cook this up for me." He said sitting down next to her. Logik had no plans on selling any of the dope in weight when Melinda finish the cooking process. He knew that he could make anywhere from forty to forty-five thousand off of the half of bird if he sold it in pieces, rather than making fifteen to twenty thousand dollars if he sold it in weight like he usually did. It would take much longer to get rid of the work selling it in pieces, but Logik needed to get his bank back up quickly. He hated that he had to start from the bottom again.

"I got'chu. But I'mma finish watching my show and go to the grocery store first." She said matter-of-factly, never taking her eyes off the TV screen. Seeing Melinda watching Jazmine's favorite TV show was starting to make him stress.

"That's wassup," He stood up. "Some more of my clothes still over here, right?" He asked, remembering how she gave him a outfit to put on after he had finished taking a shower at her house that morning she picked him up from the hotel.

She pointed towards the closet in the hallway. "Any type of clothes you ever left over here I washed and put it in the closet in the hallway." She replied in a tone that said she wanted to be left alone for the moment while her show was on. Logik had spent many nights with her in the past and left a lot of his old clothes at her house each time he changed into new ones.

He opened up the closet, searched until he found some of his clean clothes, and then made his way to the bathroom. Before he walked into the bathroom, he yelled to her. "Yo, Me-Me! I'mma kick it over here tonight too!" Me-Me was Melinda's nickname.

She put her hand up and shook it in a aggravated manner. "Whatever, boy! Lee-me-lone now, you see me tryna watch TV!" She barked. The show was getting real good at the moment because Ne Ne and Kim had just started back beefing again.

Logik shook his head and closed the bathroom door.

THE NEXT DAY, Logik was sitting behind the wheel of Melinda's Altima in Enterprise's parking lot. Melinda was inside filling out the necessary paperwork so she could rent a car for Logik.

After 30 minutes of waiting, Melinda came walking out the front door with a set of car keys in her hand. She walked over to a black Ford Focus and hopped in. Logik had told her to rent something dark and simple.

The Ford Focus was perfect.

They swapped cars a couple of blocks over at a 7 Eleven, then they both went their separate ways. Logik had hit Marcus and Budda up and told them that he was on his way to the trap. He called Jazmine's mother earlier that morning to check up on her and let her know that he had a couple of stacks to go towards funeral arrangements. But Jazmine's mother ended up cursing him out and accusing him of having something to do with her daughter's death. Right then, he knew it would be impossible for him to attend Jazmine's funeral without some bullshitting popping off between him and Jazmine's family, somebody called the police on him, or both.

Logik was about 80% sure that the police had no clue of the house he and Jazmine was leasing in the gated community. But to be on the safe side, he figured he would send Marcus or Budda over there real soon to snatch up all of his clothes. Because he damn sure wasn't going to buy any anytime soon.

As he drove to the trap house where Marcus and Budda was at, Logik decided that it was time to call Frank.

"Talk to me," Frank said soon as he hit talk on his phone.

"Yo, Frank. Wassup man, this Logik."

"I know ya voice, playboy. How you been?" Asked Frank. Really, he already knew how Logik been because Jamine's murder was all over the news.

"Man, shit fucked up homey. I gave them niggaz the muthfucking money they asked for and they still killed my shorty yo!" Logik's voice had cracked when he said that.

"Damn," Frank shook his head. Not because he felt sorry for Logik, but because he knew that Logik was about to tell him the obvious. "Sorry to hear that, playboy."

He went quiet.

"How long we talking about playa?"

Logik shrugged.

"I can't give you no specific date right now, Frank. But I am in the process of finding out who was involed in my girl's murder though. I got'chu though. Even if I gotta give you that shit in payments, I got'chu."

Silence.

"I don't do payments, playboy. What, you think I'm a loan company or summin? That wasn't a loan I gave you, Logik. That was business," Frank said referring to the interest.

"So what you tryna say, Frank?" Logik asked confusedly.

"I'm saying one week, playboy...one week."

Logik's face screwed up.

"You must ain't heard when I told you that I'm out here trying to find out who killed my shorty!?"

"And you must not heard when I said one week?" Calmly asked, but his calmness was not to be mistaken as passive.

"Yo, I been doing good business wit'chu nigga! You already know I'mma pay you your bread back got dammit!"

"This business, playa. Ain't nothing personal...one week."

Logik clenched his jaw so tight he cracked one of his tooth.

"You know what man? Fuck you nigga! Get it in blood!"

Frank snickered, "I intend to, playboy."

Then the line went dead.

Frank was a business man and he knew that a dead man can't pay what he owe. But he also was a gangsta, and his pride had meant more to him than the two hundred and sixty-five thousand dollars Logik owed him.

Logik knew that Frank was going to try and make good on his promise. Bad thing about that was that Logik didn't even know the first place to look for Frank at so he could be the first to draw blood. All he ever knew was that Frank had a house somewhere in Rockhill, South Carolina, which was almost a hour away from Charlotte.

Logik looked like a madman as he drove through the city cursing loudly and talking to himself.

Marcus, Budda, and a few of their homeboys was hanging out in the front yard when Logik pulled up. Usually Logik would've wild out on them for having so many people at the trap house. But shit had been crazy lately and maybe them having a few of their homeboys at the trap wasn't a bad idea.

Exspecially now since he had a beef with Frank.

"Logik, wassup my nigga?" A young boy name Rell spoke to Logik soonas he stepped out of the Focus. Logik threw his hand up and Rell and continued walking towards the front door.

Budda was sitting on the hood of his car talking to a few of his homeboys at the time. Marcus and Rell was standing under the big ass tree in the front yard smoking a blunt. Marcus had noticed the menacing look on Logik's face, so he told Rell to go ahead and kill the blunt, then he made his way into the trap behind Logik.

"Wassup, Big Bro? How everything turned out with the trip?"

"Everything went accordingly, man," Logik nonchalantly replied. He sat the handbag he was toating on the kitchen table and sat down. Marcus sat down as well.

Logik opened the handbag, pulled out a big Ziploc bag which had over 20 cookies of crack in it, and laid it on the table. "I want you and Budda to help me grind some of this work out. I'mma be right here trapping wit'chall niggas too though. Ya'll niggaz already got shit hot round this bitch, but I'mma have this bitch on fire soon as I hit some of my smokers up and let 'em know where I'm 'bout to be at." Logik boasted. He was going to hit up all the crack smokers he knew that head a least a thousand dollars a week habit, and let them know where he was going to be trapping at.

Since Logik decided he wasn't going to pay Frank the money he owed him. All the money that he was about to make now would go towards getting him back on his feet. He had no plans on living back in his house again. He was a "wanted man" and he needed somewhere that he was at least 90% sure he was safe from Five-O and the unknown hitmen that Frank as going to send for him. Plus, living in that house would probably drive him insane because it would remind him too much of Jazmine.

Marcus chimed in, "With all of us getting money together now, you'll have that money you owe that dude Frank in no time?"

"Fuck, Frank." Logik said hatefully.

Budda knew that it was Logik's intention to pay Frank the money he owed him, but he was now confused why Logik suddenly changed his mind about doing so? It didn't mattered to Marcus because he was down with whatever either way.

"Yeah, fuck that nigga Frank then," Marcus co-signed, piggy-backing what his big homey said.

Budda came walking into the kitchen from outside. "Damn, with all these cookies on the table, somebody will think that we 'bout to open up a bakery in this mufucka!" He said, referring to the cookies of dope that was scattered on the table.

"Yo, I'mma need one of ya'll niggaz to go to my pad and snatch up a few things for me. Ya'll already know Five-O looking for me, and I don't know if they know where my new pad at or not."

Budda sat down at the table. "A few things like what?" He asked.

"My clothes, me and Jazmine's photo album, and Jazmine's jewelry box that's in our room."

Budda shrugged. "You must be forgot you never told me or Marcus where you and Jazmine had moved to?"

Logik nodded. "You're right. I'll let you know soon as ya'll let me know which one of ya'll gone go over there?"

"Shid, I'll go get that shit now for you if you want me to?" Budda volunteered.

Logik shook his head. "Nah, bruh. It's too light outside for that right now. You can go over there later tonight sometime though."

Budda nodded his head.

Logik pulled his phone out and called JuJu, but his call was forwarded to JuJu's voicemail. He tried JuJu's number again and got the same result. He then scrolled down his contact list, found Tyreek's number and gave him a call.

Tyreek picked up on the second ring.

"Yo!"

"Sup, my nigga?" Logik spoke.

"Oh, what's the bizness, Mikey Lowrey?" Tyreek joked, referring to the nickname he gave Logik because of the many women Logik use to deal with. Mike Lowery was Will Smith's name in the movie Bad Boy, and Mike Lowrey was a playa in the movie.

"Ain't too much, Teddy Bear," Logik sarcastically replied, calling Tyreek by a nickname that Ms. Pat gave him as a youth because he was short and chubby. But as the years went by, Tyreek and grew taller and slimed down a lot. "Yo, I need you to do me a solid?" Logik asked.

"Whut'chu need, Big Bruh?"

"Ima need you to put the word out in the hood that I'm looking for some niggaz riding round in a dark-blue Malibu. Soon as you or your brother get word on that shit, then ya'll contact me at this number."

"Between me, you, and you can let JuJu know too, but the niggaz who riding round in the Malibu had summin to do with kidnapping Jazmine. Them niggaz probably ain't even riding round in that shit no more due to their come up," Logik said. "But if ya'll able to spot that shit in the hood or summin. I don't want nobody to jump the gun and try to pop off on the person driving that shit, kuz ya'll might pop off on a innocent muthfucka. Just see if motherfuckers remember seeing a dude or a few dudes riding round in a dark-blue Malibu anytime before Jazmine got killed. If ya'll niggaz find out summin, just keep tab on that shit and hit me up at this number."

"Oh word! Say no more. I'mma get on that shit A-SAP."

"No doubt. South Side, nigga!"

"All the time!"

Chapter 20

THE NEXT MORNING, Logik woke up even more tired than when he first went to sleep. He only managed to get 2 hours of sleep from the day before. The trap had ben booming non-stop, with sales pulling up around the clock. Their trap house had looked like a McDonald's drive-thru.

Logik had been telling Marcus and Budda, the night before, about a drug dealer named X-L who he said would be a nice caper for them to do. Logik didn't considered X-L a friend, but they was cool with each other. Any other time, Logik wouldn't even thought about robbing X-L. But considering his present circumstances, X-L was now fair game.

The trio had took turns taking a shower that morning, and Logik was the last one to take his. Budda had went to Logik's house the night before and scooped up all the things that he had asked for.

Logik came walking from out the back room dressed in a pair of blue 8732 jeans, a white T-shirt, a black sweater cap, and a pair of white Air Force 1's on his feet.

"One of ya'll seen my coat somewhere round here" Logik asked as he looked around the livingroom for his jacket.

"Damn, you blind as hell, bruh. You just walked past the shit," Marcus said dumbfounded, as Logik continued to look around.

Logik looked to his right ans saw that it was hanging on the back of a chair at the kitchen table. "Damn, I'm bugging." He said to himself, as he went to grab his coat.

Budda looked out the window and saw a car pulling up in the yard. Good thing they was in the country and their trailer was located on a dirt road and sat in a small open field by itself, because the type of traffic they had coming to the trap would of made any neighbor or neighbors suspicious of them.

"Look like another sale pulling up," Budda said.

"Go out there and serve them fools real quick, Budda so we can hurry up and bounce before some more muthafuckers pull up," Logik told Budda, then looked at Marcus. Hold, Budda down while he make that sale." Logik instructed before disappearing into the back room to stash the drugs.

"MAN, THAT'S A lucky ass shot!" X-L's friend, Mailman exclaimed after X-L sank two balls in the corner pocket. X-L and three of his friends stood around his stainless-steel Martin-Bauer pool table, which sat in the middle of the dining room. Stack of money was stacked along side of each other on the pool table.

X-L's baby's mother, Regina came walking into the dining room, looking fine as ever, with her hair pulled back into a bun which showed off her attractive features. Her and X-L wasn't in a relationship with each other. They only shared a son together. Actually, X-L was married and lived with his wife, but him and Regina had a bond with each other that was unbreakable.

"I'm 'bout to go pick my sister up, X-L. You and your little company need to keep that noise down before ya'll wake my baby up." She informed him before she walked off towards the living room. "And ya'll better make sure ya'll clean my damn dining room up before ya'll leave too!" She yelled, right before she walked out the front door of her apartment. X-L had set Regina and his son up with a nice apartment in a quiet mixed-community.

"She telling us to quiet down when she yelling and shit." X-L shook his head. "That girl shot the fuck out, yo."

His friend Dirty Boy laughed. "Shid, both ya'll mufuckas shot out if you ask me." Dirty Boy clowned.

"That's why ain't nobody asked you stupid nigga" Said X-L.

Regina's cell phone rang soon as she stepped into the hallway. She looked at the caller ID and saw that it was her sister. "Wassup, bitch?"

"How far you is, Gina? My feet is killing me girl?" Regina's younger sister, Latoya inquired. Latoya had just got hired at Wal-Mart

Warehouse. Her shift had ended thirty minutes ago and she was ready to go home, take a shower, and smoke some weed.

"Look, bitch, don't rush me. I'll be there when I get there. I can't wait til you save some money up and get your own car." Regina rudely told her, then ended the call. "Get on my damn nerves," She said to herself, referring to Latoya.

Regina was almost to the bottom of the stairs, when three masked men appeared from around the corner and started walking towards her. She thought about screaming, running, or just do something, but the masked men had guns in their hands and they was too close to her. She avoided looking at their faces and tried to walk past them, but the tall masked man with dreds quickly grabbed her and placed his hand over her mouth so she couldn't scream.

"How many people in the apartment bitch?" Logik whispered in her ear with a menacing growl.

Regina was in shock. She just stared straight ahead, too afraid to speak.

Logik jerked on her hair roughly. "I'mma ask you one more time. How many people in the apartment?"

She was about to answer and say five, but she thought it would be better for her son's sake that she didn't include him. "Four. It's ffour people in there," she nervously replied.

"We ain't come here to kill nobody shorty, but if you lie to me, I promise you that I'll make sure that we leave some dead bodies in that muthafucka. Now, where is everybody located at inside the apartment?"

"They all in the diningroom playing pool. I swear to you." She replied truthfully.

Logik knew that one of the neighbors could walk out of their apartments at any second, so he started walking with Regina up the stairs, with Marcus and Budda right behind him.

They stopped in front of her apartment door.

"I want you to slowly take your keys out'cho purse and open up the door," Logik demanded. "And when we get inside, don't start all that screaming. We only here to rob that nigga X-L and bounced. This don't' have to be a murder scene unless you turn it into one. You got that?" He asked.

She nodded her head obediently.

Logik took his hand off of her mouth. "Now open the door,"

Soon as the door came open, Logik shoved her inside and came rushing in after her, .45 in his hand. His cohorts followed closely behind, with their guns sweeping back and fourth. Regina yelped when Logik put his hand around her throat unexpectedly, and walked her towards, what appeared to be the dining room.

X-L leaned up off the pool table. "Ya'll heard that?" He asked his homeboys right before he was about to take a shot. He was referring to the sound Regina had made when Logik grabbed her around the throat. He was about to walk into the living room to investigate when all of a sudden, three masked men came walking into the dining room with guns drawn. He noticed that the tallest masked man with dreds had one hand around Regina's neck, and the other pointing a gun at his face.

"Ya'll know what time it is! Put ya'll hands on top of ya'lls head!" Logik commanded all four men as they rushed into the dining room.

Marcus and Budda swept their guns back and forth between the men, daring someone to move. Logik gestured with his head to Budda for him to search the four men for weapons. Budda found a gun on each of the men and tossed it on the floor by Logik's feet. Logik waited on Budda to walk back to where he and Marcus was standing at, before he looked at Marcus and gestured with is head for him to load the guns in the black duffle bag Marcus had across his shoulders.

After Marcus finished, Logik looked at X-L. "Is anyone else in this house?" Asked Logik. He disguised his voice each time he spoke because he didn't wanted X-L to recognize who he was. He had no plans on killing anyone. All he wanted was the drugs and money. But if someone was to try anything crazy, or things didn't go according to plan, then someone was sure to die.

"The only other person here is my two year old son in the backroom. He back there sleeping man, he ain't no threat to ya'll." X-L sounded pitifully.

Logik looked at Budda. "Go check it out. Make sure you serach each room thouroughly to make sure ain't nobody else hiding back there."

Budda nodded, then went and did as he was told.

"I'm telling you man, ain't nobody else..."

Logik pointed the .45 at X-L. "Shut up!" He barked, cutting X-L off in mid-sentence.

A few minutes later, Budda walked back into the diningroom carrying X-L's son in one arm and hold his .40 in the other.

"Oh, my God! Please don't..."

"Shut up, bitch before you cause your son to wake up in another world!" Logik warned her, but he was only bluffing. He wasn't into killing kids. "Give her the baby," He told Budda. Budda handed Regina her son.

X-L's three homeboys was looking at the robbers menacingly, wishing they was in a better position so they could shed some blood.

Logik walked over and sat on the edge of the pool table. He pulled a chrome silencer out of his pocket and screwed it on the barrel of his gun.

He then looked at X-L.

"We are not leaving here til we clean you out. So you can play dumb if you want to," Logik stood up in front of X-L. "Now, where the shit at?"

"It's like seven stacks on the pool table and I got about five stacks in my pocket, but other than that ain't nothin' else in here dude," X-L tried his best to convince Logik.

Logik smacked X-L with the gun across his face, sending him crashing to the floor. What was crazy is that X-L's son stayed asleep the whole time his parents was being robbed.

"You know what," Logik walked over and aimed the gun at X-L's son. "I'm tired of playing games wit'chu. Where the work at!?" Regina wrapped her arms around her son in a protecting manner. She looked over at X-L disgusted. Shocked that he would jeopardize her and his son's lives for some drugs.

"Hold up!" Regina held her hand up. "Wait!" She looked at X-L then back to Logik. "It's in back of the washer machine by the kitchen. You gotta unscrew the bolts in the back of the washer machine. I swear to God that's all that's here." Tears started streaming down her cheeks. Then she started crying uncontrollably.

By the look on X-L's face, Logik knew that they was about to hit the jackpot. He looked over at Budda and gestured with his head towards the kitchen area. "Go check it out," He kicked the duffle bag that was on the floor towards Budda. "And take that wit'cha." Budda picked the duffle bag up then disappeared around the corner. Ten minutes later, Budda came walking back into the dining room with the duffle bag. He dropped the bag on the floor and opened it up so Logik and Marcus could peep inside.

Logik looked inside the bag.

"Jackpot!" He exclaimed with a devilish grin on his face. He had saw at least 10 bricks inside of the bag. He then walked over to the pool table to collect the money. He could feel the cold stares on the men's faces, but he ignored it and focused on collecting all the money.

Budda pulled out a brand new roll of duct tape. "Yo, I'm 'bout to start taping these muthafuckas up," Budda said. "Make sure you take whatever money they got in their pockets too." Logik told Budda.

Budda collected 12 thousand dollars off of the men altogether after he finished duct taping them. When he got to Regina, he tore a long piece of tape off of the roll.

"Stop all that damn crying!" He reached out and snatched her son away from her. "Gimme this lil' mufucka!" He sat the boy on the floor and started wrapping her up with the duct tape. The boy woke up and started crying when he saw the stranger taping up his mother.

X-L looked at Logik with a sinister grin on his face.

"Mmm, mmph, mmm," X-L was trying to say something through the duct tape that was covering his mouth.

Logik didn't like the way X-L was looking at him, so he told Budda to remove the tape from his mouth briefly.

"What you got to say, fat boy?" Logik asked, looking at X-L suspiciously. He was starting to believe that X-L knew who he was.

"I ain't know me and you was on that type of time, homeboy," X-L said devilishly.

He knew who Logik was.

Logik looked at X-L with a blank expression on his face.

"Anybody ever told you you talk too much?" Logik asked him, right before he aimed his gun at X-L's mid-section and shot him several times.

The trio then left the apartment. Leaving Little X-L junior screaming at the top of his lungs, and his daddy laying on the floor leaking vital organs.

"That shit right there was too easy!" Budda said to no one in particular, as he drove his Infiniti down Hampton Avenue. Logik was in the backseat and Marcus was riding shotgun.

"Hell, yeah that shit was sweet!" Marcus co-signed. He turned around in his seat and faced Logik. "Yo, Big Bruh. If you would have been taking me and Budda wit'chu and Banks them when ya'll been on ya'll jackboy shit back in the days, me and Budda woulda been sitting on them bricks right now! Ain't that right Budda!?" Marcus asked, nudging Budda's shoulder.

"Damn, right!" Budda admitted. They was excited about the robbery they just committed. Logik felt fucked up inside. X-L was the seventh person he had killed in less than 6 months. He had no plans on taking the man's life, but X-L had knew who he was and he couldn't let him survive with knowing that. But at the same time, Logik was glad that X-L spoke up and made that knowledge known to him. Had X-L kept his mouth closed, he would of eventually caught Logik slipping in the streets.

Logik's cell phone started ringing. He saw that it was Tyreek calling him.

"Whut it is, Teddy Bear?" Logik joked.

"Sup, Mike Lowrey?" Tyreek got straight to the point. "Yo, dig this shit bruh. You need to come holla at me A-SAP my nigga. I got somebody who got some important shit to tell you about that Malibu."

"I got some shit with me I need to drop off some place first, homey. How long you think you can keep that person there with you?"

"Dude ain't round me right this second dog. You just need to come holla at this nigga now while he still here. I been tryna call you for the past hour now."

Silence.

"Where you at right now?" Asked Logik.

"We in the park."

A'ight, look, keep that fool there. I'll be there in 'bout 15 minutes."

"Say no more."

Budda looked at Logik in his rearview mirror with a confused look on his face. "Shid, where we gone be at in 15 minutes dog? We need to get all this work up out my car first man?" Budda stressed.

"Be easy Budda. Tyreek at the park with a motherfucka that got some info on that Malibu dog. I'mma just slide throught real quick, see wassup, then we out." Logik's mind was telling him to drop the drugs and shit they had with them off at the trap first. But his heart desperately wanted to know who was involved in Jazmine's murder.

So Logik decided to put his emotions before his intelligence.

Budda sighed, "I got a bad feeling bout this shit bruh, but it's your call. Where we pose to be going at?"

"They at the park in the hood." Logik replied.

Budda shook his head. "Yeah, A'ight." Budda was uncomfortable about the whole idea, but he went along with it anyways. *We just got finished doing some serious ass shit, we got a bag full of dope, and money, and some guns, and we got a murder weapon up in this bitch. This nigga Logik know damn well we need to get out of the city limits. I know you still fucked up about what happened to Jazmine and whatnot, but damn!...Mind over matter nigga.* Those were all the thoughts that ran through Budda's mind as he drove to the park on the South Side.

Marcus lit up a blunt of loud, took a few pulls, then passed it to Budda.

Chapter 21

"ONE OF YA'LL fools passed gas up in here or summin?" Tank asked covering his nose with his hand. Him, Rex, and Frisko was sitting inside a Mercury Grand Marquis with tinted windows. They was parked down the street from the Belmount Park, watching the whole area closely through their binoculars.

"Yeah, that was me," Rex confessed. "Them boiled peanuts got my stomach jacked up."

Tank turned around and looked at Rex in the backseat. "You's a stank ass nigga, man." Tank joked.

Frisko saw a Infiniti pulled up to the park and parked along the side walk. He started not to pay the Infiniti any attention because the car they was looking for was a silver Lexus. But they was ordered to "leave no stone unturned," so Frisko adjusted the lens on his binoculars and zoomed in.

"Yo, we been sitting here for the past 3 hours now waiting on dude to show his face. I say we need to ride around for a while until we spot that nigga?" Rex suggested.

"Word, that's what I'm saying," Tank co-signed.

"Nah, man. The more we seen riding round in this car, the more suspicious we look," Frisko said as he continued to watch the Infiniti through his binoculars. "But, we can bounce though and go park down the street from that bootlegger's house and watch that shit for a while?" Frisko suggested, referring to Ms. Pat's house. They was told that Ms. Pat's house was another spot they probably could catch him at.

Frisko was about to take the binocular away from his eyes and crank the car up so they could leave, but the person they was looking for had just hopped out the backseat of the Infiniti and was bobbing his way towards the park.

Frisko tapped Tank on the shoulder to get his attention.

"Yo, hold up dog! I think that's that muthafucka right there! Look," Frisko pointed. Tank and Rex put their binoculars to their eyes and followed where Frisko was pointing his finger at.

"Hell ya, hell ya, that's that nigga!" Tank excitedly agreed. Frank had put a fifty thousand dollars bounty on Logik's head, and Tank was read to earn his money.

Rex grabbed his door handle. "Come on, let's go get that muthafucka!?"

"Yo, hold the fuck up! We gone wait til that nigga walk back to that Infiniti, then we'll pull up on that fool and rock his ass to sleep.

"WASSUP MY DUDE?" Tyreek asked as Logik approached.

"Sup?" Replied Logik, bumping fist with him. "Where this nigga at you been telling me about?"

Tyreek pointed. "He right over there talking to Problem Child...Yo, Murda!" Tyreek called his name and waved him over.

"That's the due you been talking about?" Asked Logik.

Tyreek nodded.

"Yo, I now that fool. I used to fuck round with one of his cousins back in the day. Everytime you turn around though, somebody always robbing his ass," Logik clowned. "I wonder how he get a name like, Murda? Soft ass nigga should of named his self, Domestic Violence or summin?"

Tyreek chuckled. "Chill out, bruh. Here that nigga come."

"Yeah, wassup?" Murda asked , looking at Tyreek.

"This my people who wanted to holla at'chu bout them dudes in that Malibu." Tyreek told him.

"Word," He looked at Logik, "Yo, don't we know each other?" Murda asked.

"I use to fick wit'cho cousin, Shaneeka a while back."

"Yeah that's right," He extended his hand to Logik. "Long time no see. Wassup wit'chu?"

Logik shoot his hand. "Some old two-step. But yo, what you know bout them fools in that Malibu though?"

He dropped his head and shook it.

"Bitch ass niggaz robbed me bout a weeka go," He replied shamefully.

"Who? What niggaz robbed you?" Logik asked.

"It was three of them niggaz. I knew who one of them was though."

Logik remembered Jazmine telling him when she was at Subway that it was three people in the Malibu. Now, he was almost a 100% that Murda was describing the same car to him now. "Iight, well who the nigga is you say you know?" Logik was getting impatient.

"That bitch ass nigga, Peanut. That's the nigga's name."

Logik scratched his head. "Be more specific man, it's a lot of dudes name, Peanut?" Asked Logik, not wanting to believe that Murda was talking about his cousin.

"Well, this Peanut right here got a picture of a peanut tattooed on his neck."

Logik looked at Tyreek, then back to Murda. His cousin Peanut had the same tattoo in the exact same spot.

"What, you know that nigga too?" Inquired Murda, after he saw Logik's facial expression.

Logik shook his head, "Nah."

"That's all Murda. Let me holla at bruh for a minute." Said Tyreek, dismissing him. Murda bumped fist with him and walked off.

Tyreek look at Logik. "Whut'chu thinking now?" Tyreek asked. He never liked Logik's cousin Peanut, and he always knew that Peanut was a grimmey ass nigga.

Logik had a satanic look on his face. "I think Peanut got a lot of explaining to do," He replied. As of right then, the evidence against his cousin was circumstantial. There was no facts that said that the Malibu Peanut was riding in was the same Malibu that Jazmine described? And it was no facts that proved that the dudes who Jazmine said she saw in the Malibu was the same people that kidnapped and killed her? But all of the circumstantial evidence was too much of a coincident for Logik. "And that much coincidence, in the world?" Logik thought to himself.

"Oh yeah, another thing. I saw your cousin, Peanut at the Crystal Palace last night all iced out in VIP and throwing money in the air like he been Big Meech or summin. Now, I know your cousin be hustling and whatnot, but he looked like Big Meech last night in the club, real talk." Tyreek added.

"Ain't that much coincidence in the world," Thought Logik.

His head started spinning.

"Yo, I'll get up wit'chu later, Tyreek." Logik said, then stormed off with murder on his mind.

Budda wound his window down and stuck his head out so he could holla at Tyreek. "I told you them sorry as 49ers been garbage!? I bet that'll be the last time yo go against the grain nigga!?" Yelled Budda. He was a diehard Carolina Panther's fan. Tyreek had lost a $1000 bet a week ago against him on the game. That was Budda's first time seeing Tyreek since the game, so he wanted to rub the victory in Tyreek's face again. Tyreek just smiled and stuck his middle finger up at Budda.

The Grand Marquis was crawling at a low speed towards Logik.

Budda was about to stick his head back into the car, when he looked left, and saw a gun in someone's hand which was hanging out the passenger window of the Grand Marquis. He yelled Logik's name, while at the sametime grabbing his own gun.

The back window of the Grand Marquis rolled down and a arm came out.

BOC! BOC! BOC!

Rex knew his aim was off after his first three shots missed Logik, so he repositioned himself in his seat for accuracy.

Budda took aim at the driver and repeatedly squeezed the trigger. His second and third shot caught Frisko in the chest, killing him instantly. Firsko's body slmped over and his dead weight caused his foot to pressed down on the gas pedal, sending the Grand Marquis crashing into a parked car.

Logik had his gun out and was firing shots at the Grand Marquis, as he back peddled and took cover behind a tree. Marcus hopped out the passenger side with the Mausburg Pump in hand, firing rounds in the Grand Marquis as he approached it. Shots was hitting the Grand Marquis from all directions as more South Siders who was on the scene pulled their guns out and got involed.

Rex stuck his head up just in time to fire two shots at Marcus. His second shot hit Marcus high in the chest, taking him off his feet. Before Rex could make his next move, a bullet from Budda's gun spread his brains all over the back window.

Tank snatched Frisko's lifeless body and tried to use it as a shield, but the dead man was heavy as hell. Tank knew he was about to die, so he jumped out of the car so he could go out in a blaze of glory. Budda was running at him shooting wildly, but Tank got off a shot which snapped Budda's head back and sent him to the ground. So much chaos was going on that Tank never saw Logik running up on him from the side.

BOC! BOC! BOC! BOC!

All four of Logik's shot hit Tank in the back. Tank felt his body jerked, then he saw the concrete rushing his face. Logik walked up on Tank and shot him three more times for good measure. He then walked over and kneeled down besides Marcus, because he saw that Budda was already dead. Marcus was taking slow and long deep breaths.

"You gone be alright, Marcus, just keep breathing," Logik tried to comfort him as he held Marcus up in his arms. Marcus' eyes and mouth was stretched wide open as he struggled to breahe. He was in shock. "You doing good man, just keep breathing, okay?" Marcus struggled but he managed to nod his head at Logik. Logik continued to talk to Marcus, but he stopped after he realized that Marcus wasn't breathing no more. He then took his hand and shut Marcus' eyes.

Tyreek's red Chevy Capris skidded to a stop beside Logik, and the door flew open.

"Get in bruh, we gotta bounce!..Hurry the fuck up nigga!" Tyreek yelled from the driver's seat at Logik.

Logik laid Marcus on the ground and jogged to the Caprice. He held the passenger door open, about to jump in, when he remembered something. "Hold up real quick, dog!" He told Tyreek.

"Yo, nigga! Fuck that, come on!" He yelled at Logik, but he had already ran off.

When Logik made it to Budda's Infiniti, he opened the door, grabbed the black dufflebag, and ran back to the Caprice. He hopped inside then Tyreek skidded off. Leaving the onlookers on the scene observing the spectacle of death.

Tyreek drove to his grandmother, Ms. Pat's house and parked his car in her backyard. It would be another week before he drive that car again.

Melinda had been texting Logik's phone all morning reminding him that the Focus had to be returned back to the car rental place that day. The car was in her name and she damn sure didn't want to deal with Enterprise calling her about their car. Logik called Melinda while he was standing in Ms. Pat's backyard with Tyreek. When she answered, he told her to pick him up from Ms. Pat's house so she could take him to the trap in the country to pick up the Focus.

"Yo, that's it Logik. I'm bout to hit everybody up in the hood and tell'em to meet us in that field behind the graveyard. We bout to go over there on the North Side and Blaze them niggaz up." Said a angry Tyreek.

"I don't think that been them North Side niggaz that came to the park,"

"How you know that?"

"Because they know if they would've brought their ass to the park, they wasn't gone make it out of there alive." Logik stated. "Them niggaz that came out there been gunning for me. They ain't started shooting at nobody else until people starting shooting at them," He shook his head. "Nah, that was a hit right there," Logik explained. He felt guilty because he knew that Marcus and Budda was dead because of his hardheadedness and pride. Had he listened to Budda's feeling about going to the park, or had he complied with Frank's order. His two young soldiers would still be breathing. And to make matters even worse. All the drugs and money they got from robbing X-L was well over enough to pay Frank what he owned him. "Damn, man. I'm sorry ya'll." Logik said outloud, referring to Marcus and Budda.

"So what you telling me, you knew who them niggaz was that came to the park?" Tyreek asked.

Logik nodded his head.

"Okay, well who were they?"

"I don't think you know him, but his name Frank He loaned me some money so I could pay the ransom to them niggaz to get, Jazmine back."

"How much bread you owed him?"

Logik went silent for a moment.

"I owed that nigga quarter mill,"

Tyreek whistled.

"So, you basically took his bread and gave him the middle finger?" Tyreek asked the obvious.

"It ain't happened exactly like that, but yeah, that's basically what I told that fool after he started talking that tough guy shit."

Tyreek shook his head.

"Well, where he rest at so we can bomb his ass?"

Tyreek was ready to ride on Frank for sending his men to disrespect his hood the way they did.

"I don't even know, homey?" Logik shrugged his shoulders. "It's just a lot of shit going on right now dog. I'm out here tryna find these bitch ass niggaz that killed my girl and my seed, and I messed around and got two of my lil homies killed in the process." He then shook his head, not knowing what else to say about the matter.

They both sat on the hood of Tyreek's car quietly, while Logik waited on Melinda to pick him up.

Chapter 22

LOGIK GAVE MELINDA the keys to the Focus, and he hopped in her car with the duffle bag and all of his belongings.

The trap was officially closed.

They was on their way to drop off the Focus back off at Enterprise. Melinda had to be the one to drive the Focus back to the car rental place because Logik's name was not on the rental agreement forms.

Ten minutes later, he was driving down Lavania Boulevard in Melinda's Altima, as she followed behind him in the Focus. The sun was dropping low in the west and there were clouds stacking up on the southern horizon. He was emotionally drained and his eyes was bloodshot red. To Logik, it felt like someone had put a curse on him.

His mind was starting to become over shadowed by suicidal thoughts. "Jazmine, My seed, Banks, Marcus, Budda, Champagne, Sergio, Everybody! All dead because of me! My momma gone! My punk ass daddy ain't never gave a fuck about me!" His chest was heaving up and down as the tears started pouring down his cheeks. Logik was venting.

He reached inside his pants, pulled out the .40, and gripped it tightly.

"What the fuck I got to live for, huh!?" Logik put his finger on the trigger. He was only seconds away from putting the .40 to his head and blowing his brains out.

Then all of a sudden, a image of Jazmine holding a small child flashed before his eyes.

"Oh, Shit!" He shouted, slamming on the brakes. He was only inches away from ramming into the back of a mini-van at the traffic light. The image of Jazmine and the child had startled him temporarily. Not only did the image startle him, but it actually saved his life. How could he leave this earth without finding and murdering everyone who had a hand in taking the life of Jazmine and his unborn child.

Logik's sudden stop had almost caused Melinda to rear-end her own car, but she managed to stop in a nick of time.

"Boy, you better watch what the hell you doing!" She shouted loudly as if Logik could actually hear her.

Melinda remembered how she saw the pain in her cousin's eyes when she picked him up from Ms. Pat's house. When she inquired whether or not if he was okay. He went on to tell her about what happened to Marcus and Budda.

All Melinda could do was shake her head. The violent part of the street life had always made her felt some type of way.

Logik had wanted to drop all of his shit off at her house then head back into the streets to hunt Peanut down. But Melinda had begged him to stay at her house for the rest of that day so he could relax himself and collect his thoughts. He kept refusing at first, but finally ended up taking her advice.

Logik reache in the back seat, felt around inside one of his bags, and pulled out his CD case. Over the years, music had always been his outlet.

He pulled DMX's, "It's Dark And Hell Is Hot" CD out, put it into the CD player, and went to the song he really needed of hear at that time. AS he cruised the city, he was caught in a trance, as he bobbed his head to the beat and listened to DMX rapping about having a conversation with God.

As if on cue, the song ended at the sametime he was pulling into Enterprise's parking lot. He parked a few spaces away from the exit. Melinda pulled up to the office, hopped out and went inside to return the car key and collect her deposit.

Soon as she came out. She walked over to her car and stopped when she got to the driver's side. "Slide over, Jermaine. I'm driving." She told Logik, remembering how he almost had a accident earlier. They was riding dirty so getting into a car accident was the last thing that both of them needed at that time.

Thirty minutes later, Logik was sitting at Melinda's kitchen table rolling up a fat blunt of that fiyah. Keisha Cole's song "Sent From Heaven" was bumping low out of her home-stereo set in the livingroom.

Melinda was single, but she did had a dude she hooked up with from time to time. Dude was married with children like Al Bundy, but that didn't bother her one bit. She didn't needed a man cramping her style anyway.

There was one man who she really had deep feelings for since she was a young girl. But she know that her chances of fucking with him was slim to none.

Two cousins dating each other would not be a good look on the family.

"THE NUMBER YOU dialed has either changed, or is no longer in service. If you wish to..." She heard the automatic operator system said.

"Fuck!" Patience yelled into the phone then hung up. The nigga had lost his mind if he thought that he was going to get away with playing her the way that he did.

Patience and Peanut had been messing around with each other on and off for the past seven months. He dick game was weak, plus the boy was ugly as hell. But she kept him on her team because he was good for a couple of C-notes every now and then. She always knew that Peanut was a grimy ass nigga, but now she was seeing just how grimy he really was.

Patience sat on her couch looking dumbfounded.

"I shoulda known not to fuck with Peanut lame ass. I swear to God if that nigga don't give me my fucking money, Ima get someboy to kills his stupid ass!" Patience was heated. The last time she heard from Peanut was the day that him and his homeboys kidnapped Jazmine.

She folded her arms over her nice-sized breast, and sat there with a satanic look on her face as her mind drifted down memory lane.

"You stay talking that shit about Logik and Jazmine. I thought you and him suppose to be related to each other or summin?" She asked, tyring to pick Peanut's brain and figure out why he was talking about his cousin.

"Just because you and a muthafucker family don't mean ya'll stay family." Peanut hotly replied.

She nodded. "Jazmine is a stuck up ass bitch though," Patience always envied Jazmine.

"Shid, I thought you and Jazmine was cool?"

"Just because you and a bitch friends don't mean ya'll stay friends," She replied mocking his words. They was laying in bed tighter in a hotel room that Peanut rented.

Over the next couple of weeks. Patience and Peanut had saw each other almost everyday. And each time they were with each other. Peanut always had some shit to say about Logik. He always stressed to her how Logik was fake ass nigga, but Patience knew that wasn't the case.

Peanut was just plain old jealous of the boy.

One day while Peanut was talking shit about his cousin Logik and Jazmine again. A devilish plan had started developing in her mind. "You know what? I'm bout to see how far this nigga is willing to go" Patience said in her mind.

"Look. Obviously, Logik don't deal wit'chu like he used to deal with Banks and Black. I mean, ya'll cousins true indeed. But to me, it seem like he don't give a damn about that family shit," Peanuts nodded his approval.

He took the bait.

Patience knew that she had his full attention so she continued. "He riding round in a Lexus and spending money like it grow on trees, while you riding round in a fucking Maxima."

Peanut's face frowned. "Hold up bitch, what the fuck you tryna say!?" He felt offended by her comment. She put her hand on his thigh.

"Calm your ass down, fool. Ain't nobody tryna play you. I know you take care of your business out there in them streets," She said stroking his ego. "All I'm tryna say is we both know that your cousin is in a better position that you. But rather than look out for family. That nigga would rather look out for everyone else except you."

She paused. She wanted to give what she said time to marinate in to his brain before she continued. "Let me ask you summin? Would you steal money from that nigga if a opportunity ever was to present itself?"

"Damn right," Peanut replied without hesitation.

Patience smiled, then started stroking the side of his face with her hand, as she looked into his eyes. "Would you rob your cousin if the opportunity ever was to present itself?" She pressed further.

Silence. He was thinking.

Peanut's silence was starting to make Patience kind of nervous, but she relaxed when he replied, "Hell yeah,"

She then slid her hand inside his boxer shorts and pulled out his dick. "Damn you so gangsta nigga. That shit just turn me on," She said seductively, stoking his ego even more she then leaned over and started sucking his dick. Once she was finish swallowing Peanut's seed. Patience then pulled his coat to a for sure plan that would make Logik empty his pockets.

When Patience found out about what happened to Jazmine, a wave of guilt swept over her body. The girl would still be alive if it wasn't for her envious and greed. She never intended for anyone to get hurt. All she wanted was the money. Patience even made Peanut promised her that he was going to make sure everything goes according to plan. She thought that she had a "Sho nuff" do-boy on her hands. But Peanut proved her wrong.

Now Patience was sitting on her couch looking real stupid in the face. Her intuition was telling her that Peanut had shitted her out of her cut. The 500-hundred thousand dollars ransom was suppose to get split equally amoungst herself, Peanut, and his two homeboys.

Karma is a bitch! Besides. You know what they say?
"What goes around, comes around."

Chapter 23

LOGIK WAS WOKE before 9 am that next morning, but it seemed as if his body was glued to the bed.

The memorial service for Jazmine was starting in three hours, but he had no plans on going. Jazmine's family blamed him for her death and Jazmine's mother had told Logik not to bring his "Black ass" nowhere near Missionary Baptist Church. So attending Jazmine's funeral would be drama just waiting to happen.

Logik was still ducking the law and he knew that Ms. Wanda would not hesitate to contact the authorities if she saw his face. But most important, he couldn't risk getting locked up before he find out who exactly everyone was involved in Jazmine's murder. He finally made it out of bed and headed to the bathroom to take care of his morning hygiene. After he was done, he walked into the living room, where he found Melinda sitting on the couch watching TV.

"Hey,"

"Whud up," He said as he sat on the couch next to her. Melinda knew that he had a lot on his mind (especially being that Jazmine's funeral was in a couple of hours) so she chose to remain silent and continue to watch TV.

"Yo, when the last time you heard from Lisa?" Asked Logik. Lisa was Peanut's baby's mother. Melinda and Lisa was close friends with each other.

"I talked to her last night. Why?"

Logik ignored her question. "You know if Peanut was over there or not?"

"Puhleeze! That girl can't stand Peanut's ass. She don't be having him up over there like that no more."

"Ain't no need in tryna catch his bitch ass over there." He thought.

"Yo, look. I need to borrow your car again?"

Melinda sighed.

"Damn, Jermaine. You act like I ain't got shit I need to take care of too?" She understood everything that he was going through, but now she was starting to feel like he was being inconsiderate.

Logik clenched his jaw then looked at her menacingly.

"You act like you don't know what the fuck going on or sumin? You know my shit hot right now. I got muthafucking Five-O tryna snatch me up. Plus, I got niggaz tryna take my head off out here in these muthafucking streets!" He paused. "Now, like I said, I'mma need to borrow your car again?" What he said sounded more like a demand rather than a question.

Melinda just sat there with a shocked expression on her face. Her and Logik had had a few disagreements before over the years, but he never spazed out on her like the way he was now. *The fuck he gonna spaz on me about my own shit?* Melinda asked herself.

She was ready to go "straight Gangsta" on Logik but she bit her tongue. She wasn't in the mood to argue with any one else at the moment. "Look. I don't want to be arguing with your ass, Jermaine." She got up and left the room. She came back out and threw the car keys over to him, then she went back into her room and slammed the door.

As he sat there debating whether he should apologize to Melinda for spazing out on her. His mind took him someplace else. He started searching his brain for the hundredth time trying to remember every clue surrounding Peanut, and the possibility of him having something to do with Jazmine's murder. His heart wanted to give his cousin the benefit of the doubt, but it was just too many coincidental acts involving Peanut.

"Man, I know this gotta be my third time seeing that car today."

"What car, Jaz? What the car look like?"

"Ahh, it look like that car Bank's momma use to drive, but it's dark-blue though."

"This my people who wanted to holla at 'chu 'bout them niggaz in that Malibu."

"Yo, what you know bout them fools in that Malibu though?"
"It was three of them niggaz. I knew who one of them was though."
"Who the nigga is you say you know?"
"That bitch ass nigga Peanut. That's nigga's name."
"Jaz! Did they hurt you? Are you okay?"
"Yeah, I'm okay...Baby, it's Pea..."

Reality smacked Logik in the face like a ton of bricks when he replayed everything over in his mind, and he finally realized what Jazmine was trying to tell him.

"...Baby, it's Peanut!"

His face tightened and his eyes looked as if it had fire burning them. He grabbed Melinda's car keys off the couch and stormed out the front door.

The first place Logik went was to a house he knew Peanut was renting on the West Side. But he noticed a "for rent" sign posted in the front yard as he passed it moving. He rode through every spot that Peanut was known to be at. He even asked a few young kids who knew Peanut if they saw him around, but they all said they haven't seen him lately. Trying Peanut's cell phone was useless because it was out of service and everyone he called that knew Peanut claimed to not have any new number for him.

"For all I know, that faggot ass nigga probably done moved out of state or in Jamaica somewhere spending my fucking bread? But fuck all this riding around in circles looking for your ass nigga. I'mma just make your baby mamma bring you to me...Then I'mma body the both ya'll." He said outloud to himself as he rode down the block.

Twenty mintues later, he was bending a left into Eastover Apartments which was located on the Eastside of the city. Peanut's baby mamma Lisa lived in building C, so Logik parked Melinda's car in front of building A, careful not to alarm or hint Peanut of his presence when he show up later.

Logik saw a small group of guys standing in front of building B when he hopped out the car, so he pulled the brim of his cap down over his eyebrows to help conceal his identity. As he walked toward building C, he noticed that two of the guys in the group was looking at him suspiciously. Logik paid them little attention as he continued toward his destination.

Knock! Knock! Knock! Knock!

Lisa was in the kitchen frying chicken when she heard someone knocking on her front door. She wasn't expecting any company so she was puzzled as to who it was at her door.

When she looked through the peephole, she saw that it was Logik and a smile appeared on her face. Like many females, Lisa was attracted to Logik and her pussy immediately became moist when she saw his handsome face on the other side of the door. She ran her fingers through her hair in an attempt to improve her appearance before she opened the door.

"Oh, hey, Logik." She spoke. He studied her face to see if he saw any signs of suspicion.

He saw none.

"Whud up, Lisa," He started looking behind her to see if he saw anybody else in her apartment. "I'm not interrupting anything am I?"

"Oh, no. You good. I'm in here just frying me some chicken. Come on in." Replied Lisa as she turned around and went back into the kitchen. Logik walked inside the apartment and made sure he locked the door behind himself.

"So, what brought you over here!?" She yelled from the kitchen. "I hope you ain't come here looking for Peanut?" Asked Lisa.

"Actually, that's exactly why I came here," he replied as he screwed the silencer on the barrel of his Desert Eagle while walking towards the kitchen.

"Well, you came to the wrong place if you looking for him."

"Nah, I came to the right place." Said Logik, as he walked around the corner with the Desert Eagle in hand.

The fork in Lisa's hand dropped when she saw the gun and the evil look in Logik's eyes.

"Wwhat's the matter wit'chu boy?" She nervously asked, inching her way towards the frying pan that was full of cooking oil that sat on top of the stove. Logik read Lisa's mind, so he quickly snatched her up into a chokehold and placed the gun to the side of her head.

"You wasn't thinking about throwing that hot ass pot of grease on me was you?"

"No, no," She sobbed. "Why you doing this Logik? I ain't did..." her sentence was cut off when he slung her towards the living room, almost making Lisa lose her balance. When she turned around to face Logik, she was met with a fist to her eyesocket instead. Lisa crashed to the floor holding her eye. She started crawling on the floor trying to get away from Logik. He then kicked Lisa in her side with so much force that it cracked her ribcage instantly. "Awhh!" She howled in pain.

Logik went and grabbed Lisa's cell phone that was on the coffee table, walked over and kneeled down next to her. "I want you to calm yo ass down so you can call and say whatever it is you gotta say to get Peanut's ass over here." He said seriously. Her chest was heaving. "I can't even see shit, Logik. You hit me in the fucking eye, man!" She shot back angrily. She didn't know what it was that Peanut did to Logik, but whatever it was, it had to be some serious shit.

She finally calmed down enough to call Peanut. When he answered, she shot him a bullshit story about one of her male friends hitting her in front of his daughter. Even though her and Peanut wasn't fucking around with each other like that. She knew that he still oved her and would bring the pain to anyone who violated her or his daughter. Peanut told her that he was on his way and then hung up.

Lisa was one of the few people who Peanut gave his new number to when they saw each other the day before. It had shocked Lisa when

Peanut gave her $5,000 for her and his daughter. He had told her not to give his new number to nobody, and also for her not to let anyone know she saw him. She started to ask him what was wrong but decided that it would be best to mind her own business.

Even though Lisa couldn't stand Peanut's ass, the boy was still the father of her daughter. But baby daddy or not, her life was more important than his. Point blank, period.

Forty-five minutes later there was a knock at the door. Logik walked Lisa to the door with the Eagle pointed to the back of her dome. When she looked through the peephole, she confirmed with a nod that it was Peanut on the other side of the door.

"If you try some funny shit I'mma blow your brains out. You hear me?" He whispered in her ear. She nodded her head obediently then opened the door.

Soon as Peanut saw Lisa's badly bruised eye, a wave of anger swept over him. He pushed his way in the house past Lisa.

Unaware that Logik was standing on the other side of the door.

Peanut thought he seen a ghost when he turned around and saw Logik aiming a gun at his face.

"Whud up, cuzzo?" Logic said eyeing Peanut coldly.

"Yo, fam. Wassup wit all dis?" he asked, referring to the gun that was aimed directly at his face.

Lisa was standing there looking like she was about to have a panic attack. She thought about her daughter and as glad that she had let her mother pick her up the day before.

"Before I kill you, all I wanna know is why?"

Peanut chuckled, trying to play it off. "Why what? What the hell you tal—"

"Stop playing stupid nigga! You know what the fuck I'm talking about!"

Peanut raised both of his hands as if he was confused. "Cuz, I'm lost."

"Who the other niggas was that helped you kidnapped and killed my girl?"

Lisa's eyes stretched wide in shock when Logik said that. If the accusations that Logik was accusing Peanut of was true, then she knew that her chances of making it out of her current situation were very slim.

"What other niggaz!? You tripping cuz!" Peanut barked.

It sounded like a bird chirped when Logik squeezed the trigger, hitting Peanut in the shoulder.

"Ahh!" Peanut grabbed his shoulder.

"I ain't playing wit'chu fool. Who them other niggaz was!?" At that moment, Logik was thinking about all the times Jazmine tried to warn him about Peanut.

Peanut knew that Logik was going to kill him regardless of what he said. He figured that the only way he was going to preserve his life is if he killed Logik before Logik killed him.

Lisa made a sudden move, which caused Logik to divert his attention in her direction. In the split moment, Peanut pulled his gun out in one swift motion and aimed it at Logik.

"Chirp" "Chirp" "Chirp"

Logik shot Peanut three times in the chest before he was able to get off a single shot.

Peanut was dead before he hit the floor.

"Fuck!" Logik shouted angrily. He had killed Peanut before he got the info about the other people who was involved in Jazmine's murder.

"Oh my God!" Lisa shouted in fear. The scene that had just unfolded before her seemed like something out of a movie.

He turned his gun on Lisa.

"Pplease, don't kill me. I got a daughter, Logik, please." She pleaded, holding her hands out in front of her as if she could somehow stop the impact of the bullet.

Logik stood there with his gun pointed at Lisa, but was unable to make his finger squeeze the trigger. It was the fear he saw in her eyes that made him think of Jazmine and her last moments with her kidnappers.

Stop procrastinating nigga. You know you can't let this bitch live after what she just witness?

Oh. So you really ready to take another black woman's life over some shit you decided to do? Huh? When is this shit gonna end, Jermaine? The voices in his mind was telling him.

Lisa just stood there too scared to say anything else. All she kept thinking about was dying before she would get the chance to tell her mother and daughter goodbye.

And then the strangest thing happened.

Logik lowered his gun. At that moment, it didn't matter if she told the police on him or not once he leave. All he know is that he couldn't bring himself to kill Lisa, because he didn't want another Champagne on his conscience.

He stuffed the Desert Eagle back in his jeans and then left her apartment.

When he got in the parking lot, he noticed that the group of guys who was in front of the building B had disappeared. By the time he made it back to the car, he noticed that the front tire on the passenger side was flat.

"Fuck!" Logik growled, clearly frustrated. "Aye, homey. You need some help?" Said a tall dark-skinned dude with a green army fatigue outfit on and a red bandana hanging out of his back pocket, as he walked up behind Logik, catching him completely off guard.

Logik turned around. "Nah, I'm straight," He nonchalantly replied, just wanting dude to go on about his business.

He turned back around and faced the car. He was debating whether he should change getting the spare out of the trunk and changing the tire, or should he just use Pat and Charlie and get the hell off of the East side of town before Five-O arrive.

Right before Logik was about to make his decision, he felt a sharp pain in the back of his head.

Then everything faded to black.

Chapter 24

LOGIK WOKE UP with a massive headache in an empty room with his hands and feet tied to a chair. Three unfamiliar dudes was standing in front of him with menacing looks on their faces.

"Welcome back, homey," said dude with the army fatigues on, as he dropped the cigarette he was smoking on and stepped on it.

Logik realized that the dude who was speaking to him was the same dude that was talking to him in Lisa's parking lot. He wondered who the men in front of him was. He knew that they wasn't Franks' people because he would have been dead already.

"I know you looking at me and my brothers here like, 'who the fuck is these fools', right?"

"Yeah, who the fuck is ya'll?" Logik knew that whoever these dudes was that they had to be somebody who was there to kill him. So if they thought that he was going to beg them for his life, they had another thing coming.

"Who the fuck are we?" Dude looked back and forth between his brothers. "He wanna know who the fuck we are, Quick." Quick was his baby brother's name. The dude who was talking name was Jungle, and his other brother that was there with them name was KI.

Quick bit his bottom lip and looked a Logik with hatred in his eyes.

"Man, forget all that, Jungle. I'm ready to work this fool over." Said Quick as he stepped towards Logik clutching the chains in his hand. Jungle put his arm out, holding Quick back. "Hold up, my baby brother. We got pleny of time for that. Let me tell this coward ass nigga a story real quick."

Quick's lips twisted in disapproval. "If you wanna tell a story, then you need to write a fucking novel dog!" Quick angrily suggested, then he sighed. "Make that shit quick, Jungle. I'm ready to eat this nigga's food." He said impatiently.

Jungle then went on the tell Logik the story:

Ring...Ring...Ring

"Hello!"

"Wassup girl?"

"Oh, hey bitch." Replied Neitra, recognizing Champaigne's voice on the other end of the phone.

"You busy?"

"No, I'm just here polishing my toenails."

"You gone need more than nail polish to bring them crusty ass toes back." Champagne joked. Neitra was one of her friends.

Neitra sucked her teeth. "Bitch, you ain't talking bout nuttin. Wassup though?" Champagne sighed, "I called you because I need your opinion on something."

"Okay. Whuts good?"

"If a nigga was to offer you ten thousand dollars to set some other dudes up, would you do it?" She asked.

Neitra chuckled. "Bitch, that's a no-brainer. Ten thousand dollars just to set some motherfuckers up to get rob. You damn right. Show me the money nigga." Neitra confessed.

Silence.

"See that's the thing. This person I'm talking about don't wanna rob them other guys." Neitra now confused. "Well, what he wanna do then, fuck'em?" She sarcastically asked. Champagne saw nothing funny about Neitra's comment. The matter she was discussing with her was very serious. "No silly. He wanna kill them."

Neitra cleared her throat. "Wow! That's some wild shit right there girl...I don't know about that one. Not only is that some serious shit to get yourself involved in, but how you know that you can trust the nigga who tryna pay you them ten stacks? For all you know, that nigga might kill your ass after he kill them? You know how these niggaz is girl?" Neitra said, never knowing that her theory was right on target.

Champagne thought about the logic of Neitra's last statement, then shook her head. "Nah, he ain't even like that Neitra. I know for a fact Logi..." Champagne caught herself. She almost said Logik's name.

"Oh, hell nah bitch! I know damn well you ain't said Logik just now?"

"No, no. I ain't..."

"Stop lying Champagne. I heard exactly what you said." Said Neitra. "I know you feeling ol'boy and all, Champagne, but really?" She had a disappointed look on her face when she said that. "Unt-unh girl. I don't hink you need to fuck with that one."

Silence again.

"Yeah, guess you're right...Well, that's all I was calling you for girl. Let me go ahead and finish cleaning this house up some before my sister drop her two bad ass girls over here." Champagne lied. She was getting dressed for the block party. "But thanks for the advice, Neitra."

"Anytime," She replied.

"I love you girl. Bye." Champagne said, then hung up.

Neitra felt a funny feeling when Champagne said her farewell.

6 hours later, Champagne was found dead inside of her car. Neitra was sitting on the couch in her living room watching American Idol when a breaking hews interrupted the show.

The news reporter told about the killings that happened on the Westside of the city and described it as a bloody massacre. Neitra starting shaking her head from side to side as she watched the news.

The reporter then started talking about how a jogger found a woman's body slumped over in the driver seat of her car with multiple gunshot wounds to her body. Neitra almost fainted when the news reporter said that Champagne was the female that the jogger discovered.

She was in disbelief.

After Neitra calmed down, she called Champagne's sister Nae Nae, only to learn that what she had dreaded was actually a reality. She started to tell Nae Nae about Logik, and her and Champagne's last conversation but she decided against it. But she did ask Nae Nae for her brother Jungle's phone number instead.

Neitra felt that putting Logik behind bars would be too good for him. He needed to seriously get handled for killing her girl, and she knew that Champagne's brother Jungle from Watts, California would see that he get just that.

"Now you see? You killed my baby sister homey...That was our blood right there," Jungle cleched his jaw. "And you don't fuck with blood homey and live to tell about it." He assured Logik.

Quick was the first one to react. He slowly undid the chains from his fists. He reached back and swung the chains, breaking Logik's collarbone on contact. He swung again and hit him across the face, sending Logik crashing to the floor.

"Pick that bitch nigga up!" Jungle ordered. KI reached down and pulled the chair back up with Logik in it. Soon as he stepped back, Logik hawked spit in his face. "You motherfucker!" Yelled KI, as he wiped his face with the back of his hand. He then started raining blows to his head. Logik's face was a bloody mess, and his eye had swollen shut on the first hit. Three of his teeth were broken, and the inside of his lip was split wide open.

"Ahh!" KI howled in pain. He had broke his hand during his assault when it smashed into Logik's forehead.

"Watch out, watch out!" Quick said, as he pushed KI aside. Quick dropped the chains and pulled out a hunting knife. He used the knife to cut open Logik's shirt. Quick then pushed the knife into the soft skin of Logik's gut. He yanked it out viciously and cut him across the chest. Logik's chest split open like a watermelon.

Fire erupted in Logik's chest, and he cried out in pain. He felt helpless because there was no way that he could fight back or shield himself from the vicious attack.

The three men then started beating Logik like a runaway slave until they was out of breath. His face looked like someone had ran over it with a lawnmower. Logik was barely clinging to life. He was sprawled out on the floor helplessly.

Then all of a sudden he saw a powerful bright light that was getting brighter by the second. In the midst of the light, Logik could see a person (which looked to be a woman) walking towards him. Even though the blood vessels in both of his eyes was busted and he had blood in them, there was no mistaken as to who he saw walking towards him.

"Ma," Logik said in a low tone.

He noticed that his mother stopped walking when he called her name. She was dressed in a long white dress. He saw his mother looking at him with a comforting smile on her face. She then reached her hand towards Logik for him to grab it.

Logik built up enough strength to start slowly crawling towards his mother and the light. It seemed like it was taking him forever to reach her.

"Where the fuck you think you going at homey?" Jungle asked, stepping in front of Logik with a gun in his hand.

Logik's mother still had her hand out and looking at him with the same comforting smile. At that moment, Logik could feel no pain. He had no fear. The only thing he felt while laying there in his own blood, was something that he waited his whole life for.

Peace.

When he looked up at Jungle. The only thing he saw was the barrel of the gun and Jungle's finger on the trigger.

"Game over," Jungle said right before he squeezed the trigger.

POW!

Epilogue

"THAT'LL BE $83.98," the female cashier told Patience.

That night that Patience got incahoots with Peanut was the night that she had promised herself that she would never again be shopping in stores such as Rainbow's Fashion. But she broke that promise because now here she was again, shopping for cheap designer threads at Rainbow's Fashion.

She gave the clerk $84.00, grabbed her bags and left the mall.

On her way to her car, she thought about the type of lifestyle she could have been living had Peanut's grimy-ass came through with her bread. "Lying ass nigga. That's why you ass dead now." She mumbled to herself as she opened the car door.

Now that Peanut was dead. Patience knew that her chances of getting that bread was zero to none. If only she knew who those other two guys were who Peanut claimed helped him kidnap Jazmine? Maybe then could she possibly blackmail them into giving her, her share of the money.

One time in the past, Patience remembered Peanut mentioning something to her about a dude name Rambo who was supposed to be his right hand man. Patience wasn't sure if this Rambo guy was one of the dudes who aided and assisted in the kidnapping or not. But she figured that if Rambo was Peanut's right hand man, it would only make sense for Peanut to include his right hand man over anyone else in the kidnapping of Jazmine.

Patience had a homegirl who told her a few months ago (when she saw Patience and Peanut together at a gas station), that she used to date one of Peanut's homeboys.

"What's the chances of this Rambo dude being one of the ones that helped Peanut, and also being the one who Erica said she used to talk to?" She quizzically asked herself.

Patience was persistent. $125.000 wasn't the type of money the average person forgets about. If Rambo was involved, and if Rambo was the same guy who her homegirl Erica said she used to date, then she was back in the money.

That's if Rambo and the other guy allow her to manipulate them.

The palm of Patience's right hand started to itch so she took that as a sign that maybe she was about to get paid. She then started dialing Erica's phone number as she merged into traffic.

Erica picked up on the second ring.

"I don't care whut'chu want! Go sit yo ass down somewhere little boy," Erica yelled at her son, as she answered the phone. "Hello!"

"Leave my lil' boyfriend alone, Erica. You know Daequan gone be my husband when he grow up." Patience joked. Daequan was Erica's three-year old son.

"Hmmpf! Daequan better sit his little ass down somewhere before I cut it." Erica threatened.

Patience chuckled. "That boy gone be a thug just like his no good ass daddy."

"Unt'uh! Don't be talking 'bout my baby daddy." Erica said defensively and half-jokingly.

"Bitch, Puhleeze! I know damn well you ain't taking up for the no good ass baby daddy of yours?" Patience seriously asked.

"Girl, you know I been just bullshitting...Anyway, I'm glad you called."

"Oh really?" Patience known Erica for 19 years, so she already had a feeling what the girl was about the say.

Erica wanted to borrow something.

"I was gonna call you anyway and ask you, could I borrow your black pumps."

To say Patience knew how Erica thought would be an understatement.

"Bitch, you act like I only got one pair of black pumps or something?" Patience asked, feeling a little offended by Erica's stupid ass question.

"Oh, well excuse me, Ms. Diva."

"You damn right bitch, and you better know it." Patience co-signed.

"Well, since you got it like that. I might as well come over there later and pick me summin out then?"

Patience eyebrow raised.

"I don't run a clothes store bitch! Talking about you gone come over and pick summin out." She chuckled.

They both laughed at each other's comments.

"Look, I got a pair or two that I hardly wear that you can have. I'll drop 'em off to you later." Erica was a single mother with five kids, so she barely had time or money to do any shopping. "And where your ass going at anyway?"

"Oh, I met this guy last week who seemed pretty cool. He wanna take me out tonight, so you now a bitch tryna look extra cute."

"Oh, that's wassup," The main thing that was on Patience's mind at that time was getting paid. "Whatever happened to Peanut's cousin who you used to talk to? Whats-his-name?"

"Who, Rambo?"

Bingo! Patience couldn't believe how lucky she was.

"Yeah, Rambo. What happened with that?"

"Girl! That nigga a hand full, real talk."

"Rambo still be selling that good smoke right? My cousin Jeremiah tryna do some business with him." Patience lied. She had to make up something that sounded "somewhat" believable.

"Shid. He wasn't selling none when we was fucking around, but he might be doing summin now. I passed his ass on Broad Street one day pushing a black Hummer H3."

Duh! You late girl. I already knew that 'cause that's what my cousin, Jeremiah was saying." She lied again. "But anyway. What's that nigga's number so my cousin can get straight?"

"Unt'uh! That nigga ain't gone flip on me for giving out his number. Besides, I don't mess with him like that no more."

Patience snickered. "Hell, you need to be fucking with him if he balling like that, wit'cho broke ass." One of the main things Patience hated was a dumb bitch.

Erica felt offended by Patience's comment and wanted to say something, but decided to keep her thoughts to herself. She didn't want to talk herself out of two free pair of pumps.

"Whatever." She was ready to get off of the phone with Patience and her slick ass mouth. "Let me look in my phone for the number."

"You ready?"

"Yeah, go ahead." Patience stored the number in her phone then hung up.

She then begin to dial Rambo's number.

"Sup!" He said as soon as he picked up.

"This Rambo?"

"Yeah. Yo, who dis?"

"My name isn't important. All you need to know is that I know about you, Peanut, and your brother homeboy kidnapping and killing Logik's girlfriend, Jazmine."

Patience now had his full attention.

"Ya'll excuse me for a minute." Rambo told his homeboy and the two females that they was talking to as he walked back towards his car. "Yo, whoever you is bitch I don't know what the fuck you talking about." He said with a menacing growl.

"Don't play stupid nigga. I know exactly what went down. Who you think put Peanut up on game about kidnapping the bitch in the first place?" She asked. "What, you need me to go into details for you or summin?"

Rambo chose not to respond to that. For all he know, Patience could be the police.

"A hundred and twenty-five thousand dollars of that ransom money was suppose to go to me, but I guess Peanut ain't told ya'll about that, huh?"

He didn't respond.

"Nigga, I'm the one who stayed on the phone and kept ol' girl occupied while ya'll was following her all over the damn city."

Rambo remembered that day clearly. He also remembered how Peanut was texting back and forth with someone too. He was now wondering whether the girl he was talking to was the one on the phone texting Peanut that day? Whether she was or not didn't matter because Rambo had no plans on giving her a dime of his money either way it went.

"Oh, you can't talk nigga!? Maybe I need to contact the motherfucking police and let them know what ya'll did to my friend?"

"Fuck you bitch! Do whatever the fuck you feel like and when you get hit with a conspiracy charge, we'll see how gangster you is then, you stupid ass bitch." Rambo was heated. He wished that he knew who he was talking to on the phone, because he would've made sure that she wouldn't be able to say anything else to anybody ever again.

"Well, we will just see what story the police believe. Whether they gone believe a fucking career criminal, which I'm sure you are, or they gonna believe Jazmine's good friend who never even been arrested for jaywalking?"

Rambo hawked spit on the ground. For some reason Patience gave him a bad taste in his mouth. "Bitch, you bluffing."

Patience hung the phone up on him. 30 seconds later her phone rang.

"I hope you calling back to tell me you got my money, otherwise I'mma hang this phone up and drive to the police station. So go ahead and try me!" She dared. Patience had no plans on doing anything she said. This was her last move. If this didn't work, then she was out of $125,000 and she would be forced to either find a job or find some baller to pay her bills and keep her looking fly.

"Yo, calm down, shorty. You got that." He paused. "A'ight, check this out. Meet me at..."

"Unt'uh! We are not meeting on your terms. You think I'm stupid or something?" She asked but wasn't waiting on a response. "You gonna go to Shoney's on Belmont, walk in the men's bathroom, and drop my money in the trash can and leave. If it even look like you trying to post up somewhere and watch the restaurant so you can try to follow me, I promise you that I'll keep the money and still call the police and let 'em know wassup."

"Be easy, shorty. I'mma give you the money. But it ain't gonna be no damn a hunett and twenty-five stacks though. All I'mma give your ass is fifty bands and that's it. Take it or leave it."

She started to protest, but what the hell. Fifty thousand dollars was a lot more than what she had right now. "I'll take the fifty. Just make sure you do exactly what I told you to do."

A sinister smile appeared on Rambo's face "Don't worry 'bout shit. I got'chu." He promised.

Little did Patience known she was walking right into a death trap. She would never get a chance to spend or see that mean green ever again.

She set Jazmine up, now she was about to get set up. But you know what they say:

"What goes around, comes around."

Bles Shakur
About the Author:

BLES SHAKUR was born in Yonkers, New York, and raised in New Jersey, and in South Carolina. He is representing a new genre of writing which gives a reality view of life in the average urban neighborhoods across America.

Live 2 Tell was not intended to promote crimes, hate, anger, or misconduct to the reader. Rather, he wrote the novel Live 2 Tell to show the reader the flip-side of what comes with living the lifestyle of a gangsta. In order for him to grab the attention of the targeted audience he wanted to send his message to, it was necessary for him to write his fiction novel Live 2 Tell from a non-fiction perspective in order to spread his message of awakening to the youth.

Today, Bles Shakur is working on another novel and on a foundation that he started, called: "I Gotcha Back", which was designed to pay for young adults to attend technical college in their local area to earn a trade of their choice. For anyone wanting to send Bles Shakur a message, please feel free to do so by visiting him at shakurbles@gmail.com, or by writing him a short letter to: P.O. Box 1832, Sumter, SC 29151.

<u>Author's Questionnaire</u>

1. What do you think Logik's mistake was?
2. Do you think Jasmine should have ended her relationship with Logik, due to the fact that she was aware of him cheating on her?
3. How did you feel when Jazmine was murdered?
4. Do you think it was Logik's fault that Jazmine was murdered?
5. Do you think Logik was wrong for not paying Frank the money he owed him?
6. Do you believe that the lifestyle Logik lived was worth all the drama he experienced?
7. Do you think that Patience got what she deserved?
8. Do you think that Logik was wrong for killing Champagne?
9. Do you think that rappers play a major role in why young black men kill each other?
10. Could you do something positive in your community at least once a year that would bring people together for unity and peace?

<u>Acknowledgments</u>

I must have rewritten my acknowledgment a thousand times already, because I did not want to leave anyone out. But to keep everything professional, I'm now writing my acknowledgment in this fashion. So for all those whom I personally told that I would acknowledge them in my book, just know that I am also speaking of you in this acknowledgment.

First and foremost, I have to give thanks to The Creator, to my parents, and to my future wife Brittani Shakur. The only thing I have to say about about you is: *"Where were you all my life?"*

I love you all endlessly.

To my family (even the ones I have differences with), much love to you all. At the end of the day, we all we got.

Much love to all of my readers, barbershops, beauty salons, vendors, gas stations, and everyone worldwide who took the time out to read my book, support me on social media, passed my flyers out, etc., etc. I cannot begin to express how grateful I am of you.

Big SHOUT-OUT to all of my brothers and sisters who are gone, but never forgotten. May you rest in Paradise or either walk out of them prison gates ASAP.

MUCH LOVE TO DUKE CITY RADIO, TWELVE, SNAKE CHARMER, MUTOPE DUGUMA, NINO

CAPPUCCINO, llTRILL WEST, PROJECT BABIES RECORD, RADIUS RADIO, THE ROCKtheMAN RADIO SHOW, CB, AMEN RA RECORDS, SUPERIOR, MOST HATED ENTERTAINMENT, ZACHARY DIAZ (graphic designer), MARCIAL RIVERA and TAMMY RIVERA (chief editors).

To the whole BHB family: Love is love always!!

Always in solidarity, Bles Shakur.

Visit me @:
Bles Shakur@facebook.com
Bles Shakur@twitter.com
Bles Shakur@instagram.com
Bles Shakur@youtube.com
Bles Shakur@soundcloud.com
Bles Shakur@gmail.com

www.ingramcontent.com/pod-product-compliance
Lightning Source LLC
Chambersburg PA
CBHW021358150726
47989CB00005B/2298